Price of a
Bounty

S. L. Wallace

S L Wallace

ISBN 13:978-1466268104
ISBN 10:1466268107

Cover art created by Extended Imagery.
www.ExtendedImagery.com

For Jim and Alyssa

Thank you to my family and friends for their continual support and encouragement.

A special thank you to Benton Sartore, Kerstin Broockmann, Ashlee Bishop, Tim Bishop, Judith Kaplan, Monica John and James Yoho for providing honest and insightful critiques.

Prologue

I lifted the pillow and checked for a pulse. Vacant eyes gazed at the ceiling. Yes, he was gone. My work here, done.

I pulled on my black leather gloves and wiped down every hard surface I'd touched. Not that it was necessary, but one could never be too careful in this line of work.

As long as it looked like he had died of natural causes, no one would push for an investigation. And without a pending investigation, the Gov wouldn't waste resources or money on anyone, not even a member of the Elite.

He had no immediate family, and my client certainly wouldn't say anything. Even the staff would be long gone by the time anyone from the Gov arrived, especially if I left them some good pickings.

People look out for themselves – it's the nature of the beast inside.

They'd pick through his belongings, and then disappear. Someone would come looking, eventually. The Gov would send in a cleanup crew who, in addition to removing the body, would sell off any remaining assets. All proceeds would go to "benefit the Realm" which really just meant that Gov officials would receive a nice bonus.

My heels clicked on the white and gray marble tiles as I walked through the front hall. It didn't matter whether or not anyone heard me leave. They all knew he'd brought a woman home. I ran my hand through my long wavy red hair. It was time for a change.

-Keira-
Cafe de Rivoli

We show one face to our family and another to the world. *Who are we really? Who am I, and who do I want to be?* I'd been trying to figure that out ever since my father died.

My thoughts were interrupted as my target moved into view and approached The Café de Rivoli, a classy restaurant on the northwest side. Small apple trees covered in tiny white flowers surrounded the outer dining area.

The man followed the hostess inside. I walked just to the entrance and watched from the doorway. Previously, all I'd seen of him was from video surveillance and from a distance as I'd tailed him. Tonight, he wore a black pin-striped business suit. He was tall, just over six feet, and had short light brown hair. It was shorter now than it had been in the vid. I retreated back to the sidewalk and waited for a few minutes. Then it was time.

"I see my party," I said quietly to the hostess as I walked past.

"Hello, is this seat taken?" I asked, looking straight into his eyes. I could swim in the deep blue of those eyes. *Stop! No distractions, Keira, not while you're working.* "It's so busy in here tonight. There's no place to sit."

I removed my stylish pale green raincoat to reveal a flowing black skirt and pale pink top. With my left hand, I brushed back some loose strands of wavy black hair and flashed my most dazzling smile.

"It's not a problem." He gestured to the empty chair across the table. "Have we met before?"

"Does that line really work for you?" I asked with a wink.

"I have no idea what you mean." He straightened the knot of his navy blue tie.

"Separate orders please," I said when the waitress arrived. "I'll have the soup of the day and an iced tea." I needed to order light. The prices at this establishment were outrageous, especially for any dish containing meat. Meat was reserved for the Elite and the military, and by not ordering any, he would likely, and correctly, assume that I was neither.

"The orders can go on one bill," he insisted. "Chicken Kiev, a side of mixed vegetables and a bottle of your best Chardonnay." He paused, and then said, "Would you like the same?"

I looked up in surprise. Chardonnay came from Mediterra, and all imports from there were very expensive, ever since the last war. Who did he think I was? No one would pay that much for a stranger's dinner without expecting something in return, but I would play this his way for now.

"All right."

He returned his attention to the waitress. "Please cancel her previous order." He smiled at me and waited for the waitress to leave before he continued. "For whom do I have the pleasure of buying dinner?"

"Madeline Jones." I reached across the table and offered my hand as I gave him the name on the fake ID I always carried. He reciprocated with a polite handshake. It was the hand of an executive, smooth and soft, not the hand of a gardener, though I was certain I had the right man.

"Richard Burke," he said.

Yes, Richard Burke "the third" was his legal name. However, I knew that he used at least two others, Oren Johnson for example. Had I not discovered that Oren Johnson was Richard Burke III, we would not be having this conversation. I had nothing against gardeners who stole from their employers. That would make him the same as me, just another member of the Working Class.

We began to talk but paused when the wine arrived. Richard poured the drinks.

"Thank you." I picked up my glass and took a sip. "You were saying that you've lived in the city for quite a while?"

"Yes, for the past 11 years. I was 16 when we moved to Tkaron. It was during my turbulent adolescence, and I was more than a little upset about leaving all of my friends. But when your father gets a better paying job in a big city with more opportunities...well, I didn't have much of a choice. It ended up being a wise move."

I took another sip and considered him. Why had he gone undercover to steal from Elaine Ramsey, widow of the late Curtis Ramsey? When the Elite stole from each other, it was usually a maneuver meant to boost one's own interests or to take down the competition. But Burke Investments wasn't in direct competition with Ramsey Corps, and Richard hadn't stolen enough to bring them down. Burke

Investments was, in fact, what it appeared to be, an investments firm, with no ties to Ramsey Corps.

Maybe Richard had something against the military? Ramsey Corps was best known for their advanced genetic screening methods that were vital to the success of the Terenian military.

Usually my targets weren't so complex. But did that even matter? *After all, he's still Elite.*

"What about you, Madeline? Have you lived here long?"

I directed my attention back to the conversation. "All my life. My mother was from the area. She met my father when he moved here for school. They fell in love, and since they both loved the city too, they stayed. They always said it was prettier then and cleaner."

I finished my first glass of wine, and Richard poured me a second as our food arrived.

"What's your father's line of work?" he asked.

"Was...my father was an architect." I'd learned it was easier to remember lies when I intertwined them with the truth. My father really was an architect. He'd designed buildings of beauty and grace. Though time and pollution had done their work, the buildings remained a testament to the achievements of our citizens, a dream of what our city could once again become. My parents had such wonderful dreams for us.

I glanced away as I remembered my father and mourned the loss of those dreams. If I could convince Richard to worry about me, if only a little, it may be a way in. The tears in the corners of my eyes were genuine as I thought about my father. He never should have died that way. There was no reason for it!

Richard studied me intently. "I'm sorry." Then he tactfully changed the subject. "What do you do, Madeline? How do you spend your days?"

"I'm a maid at the Beckett estate," I lied. "I clean mostly, but sometimes I'm asked to run errands or watch the girls when the nanny is out."

The Beckett's were exceedingly wealthy, and Lance Beckett was as corrupt as a man could be. He would do whatever it took to keep his social standing and had earned himself many enemies along the way. It was a wonder I hadn't been hired to take him out yet.

I'd almost finished my second glass of wine. Richard picked up the bottle and offered me some more. "How long have you worked for the Becketts?"

He was fishing for information, and again I wondered why. And how did the Becketts fit in?

Keep your head in the game. If Beckett is your way in, then so be it.

I drank my third glass of wine more quickly as I replied, "I've been working there just under two years." That was long enough for me to have accumulated some important information.

"And do you live on site?"

"Of course." I could pull this off. My sister worked at the Beckett estate. I could offer as many details as he needed, but now wasn't the time. If I gave Richard too much information too quickly, there would be no reason for him to keep me around. It was time to redirect the conversation.

"What do you do for a living, Richard?" I already knew the answer to that. Richard was the vice president of his father's investment firm. He'd never had to really work for anything in his life.

"I work with investments." His voice was cool and

calm, but the look in his eyes was one of growing suspicion.

I stretched my arms and yawned. "It's getting late, and I'll have to get up early for work tomorrow. I should be going. Thank you very much for dinner and for your company." As I stood, I made sure to stumble.

Richard jumped up to steady me. "Please, let my driver take you home." He stood and helped me with my coat, then paused to pay the bill and place a call to his chauffeur.

I reached for his arm as we walked out the door together, and Richard led me to a sleek silver automobile that pulled up in front of the Café de Rivoli. I climbed in, impressed with the vehicle. This piece of old techno looked like it wouldn't break down on the ride home. The upkeep must cost a fortune!

I simply said, "Nice." Then I snuggled up next to Richard and pretended to fall asleep.

"Madeline?"

I made sure my breathing was even and let out a little sigh.

"We'd better not take her back in this condition," he said to the driver. "Take us home."

We soon arrived at an apartment that had been rented to a gardener named Oren Johnson. I wondered briefly if Richard's father knew about this apartment. Probably not. I let him wake me just enough to guide me into the building. He led me to the elevator which whisked us up to the eighth floor.

When Richard opened the door to the apartment, I stumbled directly to a black leather couch and fell upon it. He picked me up and carried me into the bedroom. He gently placed me on the bed, removed my coat and shoes, then covered me with a downy comforter. Quietly, he returned to the living room and left the door ajar.

I held still and kept my eyes closed while I remembered the layout of the room. The door to the living room was just ahead and to the left. A large window that overlooked the cityscape was off to my right. A dark mahogany dresser stretched along the wall across from the bed and next to the door. The entrance to a large closet was on the far left next to a door to the master bath.

I'd cracked the safe in the closet a couple of days ago when I'd done a preliminary check of the apartment. The stolen gats were there, but it had been too soon. The money had certainly been tempting, but that wasn't the whole job.

I heard Richard's voice from the living room, one side of a conversation. Only the Elite could afford high techno devices such as personal transceivers, televiews and home security systems. I listened carefully.

"No, you shouldn't come over tonight... I'm just tired... Well alright, if you're already in the neighborhood." He moved toward the bedroom and closed the door.

Immediately, I threw back the deep blue comforter, climbed out of bed and opened the safe. Inside was a handgun – guns weren't my style. In my opinion, they left too much evidence behind, so I didn't even touch it. I also found a gold pendant with a ruby, beautiful and expensive. Neither were what I'd come for, so I closed and locked the safe. I quickly scanned the rest of the closet. Where had he put the money, and why had he moved it?

I checked the master bath, a room I'd only

glanced into before. I didn't really expect to find the gats hidden in there, but I needed to make sure. The room was classy and clean. The decor, black and white with polished silver hardware. And also, a whirlpool bath. I'd heard of them but this was the first one I'd ever seen.

A knock from across the apartment caught my attention, followed by a woman's voice, sugary sweet. "Hi, Oren! How was work?"

I moved closer to the bedroom door so that I wouldn't miss anything. I guessed he was talking to Rose, his current girlfriend, an Elite socialite. I only knew of her because of my surveillance. She really wasn't my concern. I remained quiet. It would be best that she not find me here.

Whatever they were doing, they did quietly for quite awhile. Then Richard said, "Is your driver waiting?"

"No, silly. Then my father would know I was here. My driver is still with the car back at Angelina's."

"How did you?"

"I gave him the slip, and I walked. It really wasn't that far. But now that you mention it, it is late. Maybe I should stay. You know, a girl shouldn't be out on the streets all alone, especially at this time of night."

"And have your father call the police...again? And anyway, I've had a long day. I'm exhausted. I'll call my friend, Eberhardt. He can give you a ride home."

"Have you thought about what I said? About getting a car of your own, now that you have the means?"

"No, not yet."

Interesting! Why hadn't he told her his real name

or that he had a car as well as a chauffeur? *There seems to be more to you, Mr. Burke, than even I've uncovered.*

"Wait, Oren. There is one more tiny thing...I need a little cash for the rent," Rose said.

"How much do you need?"

"3,000 gats, and I'd rather not ask my father for it." As the sound of her footsteps approached the door, I backed up and moved toward the bed. I could hide, but then Richard would wonder why I wasn't where he'd left me.

"Wait, Rose. I don't keep that much in the apartment, but I can get it for you. I'll stop by tomorrow afternoon."

Did she really believe he was a gardener who wore a suit, and who had enough money that he could loan her 3,000 gats for the rent?

"Oren, I have a fabulous idea," she gushed. "I could move in with you! Then we wouldn't have to pay twice the rent, and I could help you relax after a stressful day in the sun."

"Something to talk about another time," Richard said gently. "Let me walk you to the car."

"Couldn't you just borrow your friend's car and drive me home yourself?"

"He usually doesn't let anyone else drive it, and as I've already explained, I'm exhausted. I shouldn't drive right now."

When I heard the front door close, I cracked open the bedroom door. The plush cream carpeting gave way to a smooth polished hardwood floor. I'd have to step quietly. Quickly, I searched for the missing gats.

In the front closet, I found Richard's pin-striped business suit. Had he transformed into Oren the gardener for Rose?

I checked through his desk and found an account booklet for Richard Burke III. The missing money wasn't listed as a recent deposit.

Could he have more than one account? No. He has another apartment.

I hurried back to the bedroom and closed the door behind me just as Richard reentered the apartment. I returned to the bed and covered myself with the comforter. Then I waited for the apartment to settle into the quiet of the night.

My job had become more difficult. My plan had been to make contact and convince Richard to take me home. I knew he wouldn't risk taking me to his other apartment. That was good because in addition to Elaine Ramsey hiring me to take out Oren, not Richard, the stolen gats were also here, or at least they had been here the last time I'd checked. Then, I planned to kill him in his sleep and leave with the money as well as anything else of value. The only loose end would have been the driver, Eberhardt. He knew what I looked like, but I wasn't worried about that. I was skilled at transforming my looks.

Now, I needed a new plan. How could I retrieve the money from Richard's other apartment, the one with high techno security, yet kill him here in "Oren's" apartment? It had to be that way or Ramsey would know. As soon as it hit the newsvids, she would realize that Oren was Richard, a member of the Elite. If I killed him there she would know that I'd held back information. That wouldn't do. I'd have to convince Richard to keep me around longer, to trust me, until I could find a way.

I stretched and wondered where he would sleep tonight. Most men would have chosen the bedroom with me, but Richard had been such a gentleman throughout the evening that I suspected he would sleep on the couch. Time passed. Richard didn't return.

-Guy-
Who is Madeline?

A mysterious young woman recently entered my life. I noticed her the second she walked into the café and was pleasantly surprised when she walked directly to my table. I immediately wondered why – why had she come to me? Did she know who I really was? If so, what kind of help was she seeking? She introduced herself as Madeline.

Madeline had the most amazing green eyes. She was well dressed yet looked hungry. Despite her clothing, I knew she wasn't Elite. I could also sense that she needed something, possibly food, probably something else. She must know, but who directed her to me?

I ordered my favorite, Chicken Kiev, a side of mixed vegetables and a bottle of Chardonnay. Then I hesitated. She really did look hungry.

"Would you like the same?" If she saw that I was willing and able to offer this, it might put her at ease. I was well aware that asking for help could be a daunting task, and I wanted to make this as easy as possible for her.

But, she didn't ask. Not then, and not as the conversation continued. In between topics, Madeline seemed to be studying me. Was she trying to decide if she could trust me? I wanted to ask, "Why did you approach me?" but instead said, "What do you do, Madeline? How do you spend your days?" Maybe her answer to that would provide some clues.

When she asked, "What do you do for a living, Richard?" I realized she wasn't going to ask for help. So why was she there, at my table? She had obviously sought me out specifically. But why?

I did discover the answer to my question but not until later that night. Madeline drank too quickly, or pretended to do so, and I ended up taking her home to see how this would all play out. I meant to keep a close eye on her.

Unfortunately, I hadn't anticipated Rose. Neither her friends nor her family knew we were seeing each other. After Rose left, I waited to be certain that Madeline was sound asleep before I opened the safe. I could help Rose a little. It was the least I could do before ending the relationship.

All of the money was gone, every last gat. So that's what Madeline had wanted, and she took the opportunity when I walked Rose to Eberhardt's apartment. But, why was she still here? I immediately checked her purse and coat pockets and discovered a set of keys, an ID issued to Madeline Jones, 24 gats, two tubes of lipstick, a travel toothbrush and a couple of... I shook my head. Was that how she made a living? That and stealing?

Why did she carry two tubes of lipstick? Different colors perhaps? I opened them. Small metal rods poked out of one, a lock pick kit.

Who is Madeline? How did she know about the money? Where did she put it? Why is she still here? More important, what else does she know? I couldn't leave her unattended, not now.

As I watched her sleep, I replayed the evening in my mind. I wondered if any of the details she'd shared about her life and family were true. When I'd asked about her father, her reaction had seemed genuine, but what about the rest? Did she really work for the Becketts? Should their estate be a future target? We could always use more funding, and I was sure I could uncover a good reason for Lance Beckett to "donate" to the cause.

My thoughts drifted back to Madeline, to her long wavy black hair and her bright emerald green eyes, eyes that had seemed familiar. I'd been serious when I'd asked her if we'd met before, but I didn't recognize her name.

Eventually, I grew tired. I called Eberhardt and asked him to watch our "guest" through the night.

-Keira-
Friend or Foe?

I blinked. Sunlight streamed through the bedroom window, but a shadow fell over the bed. A large muscular man sat in a straight-backed chair. He stared at me. I stared back.

"Aren't you Richard's driver?" I feigned an indignant tone. "Why are you watching me?"

Eberhardt ignored me but called out. "Rick! The girl is awake."

Richard III entered the room. He appeared rested and ready for the day in a tailor-made light grey business suit.

Why am I being guarded? Is he onto me? I looked past him. The closet door stood open, as did the door of the safe. *Oh, hell!*

"Good morning, Sunshine! So, where did you put it?"

"What?" I asked in confusion. "Where did I put what?"

"My money. You bat your eyes, pretend to get drunk, end up at my place and steal my money."

"I honestly don't know what you mean." My eyes grew wide.

"You know something though."

I knew something all right – I'd been set up. *The money isn't at his other apartment. It isn't here because someone else has already gotten to it.*

Could it be Rose? Although they hadn't been together long, Rose could already have a key to the apartment. Had she really needed to borrow money for rent, or was that just a cover story to direct attention away from herself? But, how had she opened the safe on her own? I hadn't looked into her background much. Had I missed something crucial? I thought she was a fluffy headed socialite. Why she was interested in a gardener, I had no idea. Did she know he'd been lying to her? If so, and this was about money, why hadn't she just blackmailed him?

Who else? Eberhardt probably knew about the money. He'd been employed by Richard for over a year, and they seemed close. He drove Richard to his father's firm as well as to his other "side jobs." But if Eberhardt was going to steal from Richard, wouldn't he have done so long before now?

Are Rose and Eberhardt working together? I glanced at Eberhardt and realized he had the look of a professional bodyguard. He moved away from the chair and stood imposingly in front of the door. His body language said there would be no escape. He was a big, scary-looking man in a suit, tall with wide shoulders, muscular, with a scar across his left cheek. He was the kind of man who looked like he meant business, the kind of man I didn't want to cross, if I could help it. My gut told me that Eberhardt had, and always would have, Richard's back.

I realized then that there was one other person who could have orchestrated this. *She wouldn't have double-booked, would she? Is she crazy? Doesn't she realize who she's messing with?*

Richard turned the chair around and sat down. Casually, he leaned his arms across the back of it and faced me. I swung my legs over the edge of the bed and sat up straight. I looked directly into his eyes, showing no fear, and dropped the innocent act.

"Who are you, Madeline?" Richard asked.

I responded with a question of my own. "Why haven't you told Rose the truth?"

"That's none of your business. Who are you?"

"That depends."

Richard shook his head. "Depends on what?"

I softened my tone. "What's the money for?"

He looked at me steadily for a moment, calculating, and then shared just a little. "All right, that money was meant to help people, the sick, the needy, those the Elite step upon or push out of the way. People like your father, I suspect."

I felt a catch in my throat. Could he possibly understand? Why did he refer to the Elite as if he wasn't one of them? Wasn't Richard the type of person who stepped on people to get ahead? Weren't they all?

The last war created the Divide among our people. The Elite and those they considered useful received money, medicine and care. They didn't just survive; they lived. However selfishly, they lived, and everyone else...

I thought Richard was one of them. I wouldn't have taken the job if I'd thought otherwise. Why would he be interested in people like my father? Artists and dreamers, idealists. Hell, everyone who wasn't a member of the Elite, was either used or left to rot and die.

I thought for a minute longer while Richard

waited patiently for me to make the next move. Elaine Ramsey was on one side of the Divide. I was on the other. Which side of the Divide was Richard on?

Ramsey had hired me to find and return her money, and in the process, eliminate Oren Johnson, a gardener, a nobody. If she'd known who he really was, she wouldn't have ordered a kill, not for the amount he'd stolen. The Elite wouldn't hesitate to squash those beneath them for touching their precious gats, but they'd never hire a Freelancer to kill one of their own, not unless the stakes were much higher. *Maybe the stakes are higher than I thought.*

I'd never had a problem eliminating the wealthy and corrupt. In my experience, the two went hand in hand. I believed my job made Tkaron a safer city. But, I never took out the innocent or downtrodden. Those were the people I wanted to help.

But now... I realized now that Richard hadn't given me any reason to believe that Tkaron, or even the entire Realm of Terene, would be better off without him. And based upon what he'd just said, the opposite could be true.

All right, if she's changing the rules, then so am I. I took a deep breath and hoped I wouldn't regret what I was about to say.

"Elaine Ramsey hired me to retrieve her money and eliminate you." Call me a fool, but telling him felt right.

Out of the corner of my eye, I saw his bodyguard, pull out a gun. Richard motioned for him to hold back and quietly said, "Eberhardt doesn't respond well to attempts on my life." He hesitated for just a moment. "What do you know?"

"I know that Richard Burke III is your real name and Oren Johnson isn't."

"Is that all?"

Eberhardt held his position. I hadn't given them enough.

"There's more, and I'll tell you when he lowers the gun."

Richard looked at his bodyguard and nodded. Eberhardt lowered the gun and clicked the safety into place.

"You're Guy Bensen," I said.

Now it was his turn for silence. My contact had assured me that this alone was what was most important about Richard Burke III.

He narrowed his eyes. "Does Elaine Ramsey know about my ties to the Resistance?"

"She never mentioned it."

"She only hired you because of the money?"

"Yes."

"Then you learned about me all on your own."

"Yes."

Richard was a member of the Resistance. He had just confirmed it. My source had neglected to mention that. It was the game we played. If I hadn't been so evasive about what I was going to do with the information, she may have told me more.

"Madeline, you're very good at your job."

"You have no idea."

"We could use your talents."

Me, fight for the Resistance? Their goal was to return balance to our society. I believed it was a losing battle yet hoped I was wrong. It surprised me that someone as wealthy as Burke was involved.

"I live between the light and the dark," I said. "The dark usually pays better and generally seeks to eliminate itself anyway, but maybe I can be of some assistance."

"You can begin by returning the money."

"I would if I could," I responded honestly. "It was already gone when I got here."

"I don't believe that. The money is the only thing missing. If someone else had broken in, don't you think they would have taken more? Is your arrival the very same night just a coincidence?"

"No, I don't think so."

Richard closed his eyes. "Are you willing to take a lie detect?"

"I don't really trust old techno."

"Don't worry, my lie detect works every time."

"What do you mean?"

"Eberhardt will break one of your fingers every time I suspect you're lying to me."

Eberhardt holstered the gun beneath his suit coat, flexed his fingers and smiled at me. At least I think it was meant to be a smile – it came across as more of a grimace.

Richard looked directly into my eyes. "So... are you ready to begin?"

I couldn't quite read his expression. *Is he serious, or is he bluffing?* He held my gaze. *Do I even have a choice? Either I accept his offer and hope he believes me, or I don't and...and what?* I knew what I would do in a similar situation. In their eyes, I was a threat to the Resistance, and Eberhardt had a gun that I was certain he was willing to use. I would have to convince them that their secret was safe with me, that I could be trusted as an ally. My life depended on it.

I steadied my gaze and my voice. "Sure."

Richard walked over to the dresser. As he opened

the bottom drawer and pulled out an old fashioned lie detect, I quietly sighed with relief.

He turned to me. "Is there anything you need before we begin? This will be more reliable if you're relaxed."

"Mouthwash or toothpaste – morning breath," I explained with a shrug.

Richard nodded toward the bathroom. "In the medicine cabinet."

After I took care of business, I located the mouthwash, mint flavored, sipped some and began to swish. I gazed into the mirror over the ebony sink. A slender young woman with long wavy black hair and emerald green eyes framed by long dark lashes gazed back at me. I spat into the sink, and then glanced over at the whirlpool bath.

Well, now that I had some time. It was black and shiny. I ran my fingers along the edge, clean. I hadn't seen anything like this, well, ever. Working Class apartments had tubs stained by mineral deposits. I turned one faucet, cold, then the other, hot – a rare commodity! If this ended up being my last day ever, I was going to make it a good one, and if it wasn't...well, a hot bath certainly wouldn't hurt. When the water was high, I removed my clothes, lowered myself into the tub and pushed a button that started the jets. The tension drained away as I enjoyed the first hot bath of my life.

My eyelids fluttered open when I heard knock on the door. It opened, and Richard poked his head inside. I made no move to cover myself but just looked at him, then leaned my head back, closed my eyes and sighed.

About an hour later, I exited the bathroom. I felt refreshed and confident. I'd blown my cover, and I was still alive, at least for the moment. Richard and Eberhardt were in the living room. They stared at me for a minute.

Then Richard stood and asked, "Are you ready?"

"That tub is one piece of old techno I could get used to! You did say this will work better if I'm relaxed," I reminded him.

Richard ignored my comments and simply pointed to a chair. I sat, and he began to connect me to the machine.

"I'll ask you questions. This part," he pointed, "will record my questions and your answers. The electrodes," he indicated some wires, "will send signals to these needles which will make marks on this paper. Truthful answers will leave different marks than false ones, so I'll begin by asking you some questions we both know the answers to. Are you ready to begin?"

"Are you sure this thing is reliable?"

Again, he ignored my comment, and the interrogation began. "Where did we first meet?"

"At the Café de Rivoli, downtown. We had dinner together."

"Who hired you?"

"Elaine Ramsey."

"What is my name?"

"Your birth name is Richard Burke III. You also go by Oren Johnson, but you prefer Guy Bensen, at least with people you trust."

"What do you do for a living?"

"I'm a Freelancer." I saw no need to lie about this, not now.

Richard paused and shook his head.

"Does Elaine Ramsey know about my ties to the Resistance?"

"I don't think so, but maybe."

"Is Madeline Jones your real name?"

Finally, something new. "No, I'm Keira Maddock."

-Guy-
The Lie Detect

The next morning, I awoke early as usual and prepared for the day. Finally, Eberhardt called, "Rick! The girl is awake."

When I entered the bedroom, I noticed that Madeline's eyes went directly to the open safe. Just as I'd expected! Then she looked at Eberhardt and seemed to realize something.

It was troubling that she knew me as Guy Bensen, especially since she was working for Elaine Ramsey. Most people who used my code name worked with me or needed my help. Madeline fell into neither category, and I feared that she knew too much. I needed to know exactly how much. It was time to use the lie detect.

"I don't really trust old techno," she said.

"Don't worry, my lie detect works every time."

"What do you mean?"

With a straight face, I said, "Eberhardt will break one of your fingers every time I suspect you're lying."

Eberhardt played along. He put away the gun, flexed his fingers and smiled at me. I smiled back.

"So...are you ready to begin?" I asked Madeline.

"Sure," she said.

Was she a masochist, or was she calling my bluff? I looked at her more closely then, and for the first time, I noticed a scar on her right forearm, an old knife wound perhaps. The sleeve covering her left shoulder had slipped down, and I could see another scar, an old burn in the shape of a circle. There was also a thin line of white scar tissue above her left eyebrow.

I reached into the bottom dresser drawer and pulled out an old fashioned lie detect, then turned to her.

"Is there anything you need before we begin? This will be more reliable if you're relaxed."

"Mouthwash or toothpaste."

She probably needed the bathroom for more than that after the amount of liquid she'd consumed the night before. I nodded in the direction of the bathroom.

Eberhardt looked at me and raised his eyebrows when we heard running water.

"Really?" he asked.

I shrugged. "As long as she doesn't leave before we have time to question her. I'll make sure she's not trying to sneak out the window."

I rapped twice on the door, then opened it. Madeline was clearly enjoying a hot bath, and she made no move to cover herself. It took some effort, but I pulled my head back, took a deep breath and motioned for Eberhardt to follow me into the living room.

Eventually, Madeline emerged from the bathroom, wearing her skirt and pink top. Wet hair only enhanced her beauty. It would be pertinent for me to remain cautious. I realized that I was staring again and forced myself to look away. *Her eyes! She looks almost like...*

"Are you ready to begin?" I asked and turned my attention to the lie detect.

What was I going to do with her? She knew I was part of the Resistance; she was a liability. It would be disastrous if Elaine Ramsey learned about that. I needed to determine exactly what Madeline knew. Then I'd have to convince her not to talk – either that or Eberhardt would have to...I couldn't let it come to that.

My first questions established how honest answers would be recorded.

"Does Elaine Ramsey know about my ties to the Resistance?"

She said, "I don't think so, but maybe."

The lie detect confirmed what she'd told me earlier. Nevertheless, Ramsey would remain a threat as long as she believed Oren Johnson was alive. What was Madeline planning to tell her? For that matter, was her name really Madeline?

"Is Madeline Jones your real name?"

"No, I'm Keira Maddock." The lie detect recorded this as truth. The resemblance was clear.

"Are you related to Scott Maddock?"

She looked surprised and responded with a question instead of an answer. "How do you know Scott?"

That changed everything. I turned off the machine and the recorder and reached over to gently remove an electrode. She reached up and removed the others.

"You don't have the money, do you?" I looked directly into her eyes. "It was already gone when you got here."

"Yes, it was gone," she replied without looking away. "I was planning to steal it from you, but when I opened the safe, it wasn't there. Killing you prematurely would have only made the rest of my job more difficult." She finished with a shrug.

Her indifference sent a shiver down my spine. She and Scott looked so similar yet were undoubtedly different.

"How do you know Scott?" she asked again.

Even so...I ignored her question, reached into a small bag and extracted a magnet. I picked up the recording cassette. "There will be no record of our conversation."

I looked toward the door. "Eberhardt, please run out and pick up some breakfast for all of us." I returned my gaze to Keira. "We have a lot to discuss."

Before he left, Eberhardt walked over and handed me his gun. He knew I'd never use it, but Keira didn't know that.

After he left, I placed the gun on the table in front of me and answered Keira's question with a half truth. "Scott is one of my clients."

She narrowed her eyes. "Maybe, but there's more. How do you really know him?"

This was not where I'd expected the conversation to go when I'd suggested the lie dectect. How much had Scott told her?

"I met Scott when I first moved to Tkaron. We were in somewhat similar situations. He worried about you and your sister and wanted you to be safe and happy. Are you?"

"As much as can be expected. I can take care of myself if that's what you're really asking."

"Scott believes in the Motto of the Realm. Do

you?"

"Reliance on citizens makes us great," she said bitterly. "That used to mean all of us, working together, to better the whole."

"Not a few at the top relying on the rest," I completed her thought. "Yes Keira, I prefer the original meaning too. Earlier you implied that you didn't think it was a coincidence the money disappeared last night. Who do you suspect?"

"Eberhardt appears to have the know-how," she began, but then hesitated.

"No." I shook my head. "Some of this money was earmarked for his family. Any other ideas?"

"How well do you know Rose? Don't you think it's interesting that she asked you for a large sum of money when I was in the very next room? Maybe she wanted you to suspect me."

I thought about that. "Possibly. She's greedy, but she's also a terrible liar, and had she known you were here, I think she would have been jealous of another woman in my bed."

I continued to think about it. Had Rose ever been near me when I'd opened the safe? Yes, she had been standing behind me when I put her mother's pendant in there for safekeeping. Why did she ask me to keep it? I hadn't kept a close eye on her every time she'd visited because everything important was locked up or hidden away.

"She's had the opportunity," I shared, "but she's not cunning enough to have planned something like this."

"I know someone who is. I think Elaine Ramsey has already retrieved her money, and I believe she hired Rose to do that."

"She hired you to do that," I said.

"I think she wanted me to believe that."

"But why would Rose turn on me?" I wondered aloud.

"You already answered that. 'Rose is greedy,' you said. And she was dating a lowly gardener. Why?"

"I met her when I was working undercover at her father's estate. I decided she would be a more valuable asset than what I'd been planning to steal."

"You misunderstood my question. Why would a rich girl date a gardener, and how did you ever convince her that Oren could afford a place like this anyway?"

"I told her I'd recently received a large inheritance from my uncle."

"You've only told her lies. She doesn't even know your real name." She nodded. "That was good thinking. If Ramsey has been in contact with Rose, your lies will probably end up saving you."

Keira was right – I'd never trusted Rose. We'd been doomed from the start. She had every reason to turn on me.

"Richard, retrieving the money was only part of the job, and there is no way Ramsey would have convinced Rose to kill you, not someone like her – that's my job. We need to make it look like I killed Oren Johnson. It's the only way you'll be safe."

I narrowed my eyes. "No, we're talking about your safety. However, I believe we can come to an agreement. If Elaine Ramsey believes Oren Johnson is dead, she may leave us both alone."

-Scott-
Introducing Elaine Ramsey

I was 16, the age of Eligibility, when I joined the military. It didn't matter that I hadn't completed my traditional schooling. The military took care of its own, and all training would be provided. I knew it would be a lifelong commitment to a Gov I didn't agree with most of the time, but given the circumstances, I couldn't really think of a better option.

Those who enlisted were given special tests. The doctors were pleased with my results. They said I would be an asset to the realm and registered me for the special operations regiment.

I left home with high hopes. I would have a job. I would be able to contribute to society. Better yet, I would be able to help my family. Members of the SOR received extra provisions. I'd immediately requested that my extras be sent home to help my sisters who always had so little.

***

A few weeks ago, Mrs. Elaine Ramsey requested a meeting with the Lieutenant General. She also requested that I sit in as a witness. It was a common practice, though why she requested me specifically, I had no idea, and I didn't ask. No one ever questioned the head of Ramsey Corps, a tall and thin yet foreboding elderly woman. Near the end of the meeting she shared a personal concern.

"General, I'm embarrassed to say that I was recently robbed."

The general glanced at me and seemed to consider his words carefully before he spoke. "I hope whatever was taken wasn't...invaluable."

"No, but it was a lot of money, and I would like it back. I was thinking maybe we could send in some of the soldiers, discreetly."

"If our office gets involved, I'll have to report it as part of the public record. Would you still like our help?"

"No, thank you," she replied as she shook his hand. "I'll find another way."

"Right this way, Mrs. Ramsey." I held open the door for her. "I'll be happy to escort you to your car."

After we'd left the building but before we reached her car, I continued quietly, "I know someone who is in the business of solving problems discreetly and off the record."

"I'm interested." She smiled.

"There would be a cost for her services."

"Cost is not an issue, soldier, if the work is of good quality."

So I gave her Keira's alias and told her she should expect to hear from Madeline within the next few days. I'd never approved of my sister's choice of occupation, yet I tried to help her out whenever an opportunity presented itself.

-Keira-
Getting Out

"Richard, retrieving the money was only part of the job, and there is no way Ramsey would have convinced Rose to kill you, not someone like her – that's my job. We need to make it look like I killed Oren Johnson. It's the only way you'll be safe."

"No, we're talking about your safety. However, I believe we can come to an agreement. If Elaine Ramsey believes Oren Johnson is dead, she may leave us both alone."

I nodded. All right then, we understood each other. "By the way, what do you want me to call you?"

"Most people call me Richard. My friends call me Rick."

"And you prefer Guy but only with people who know your secret." I paused for a beat, and then asked, "What does Scott call you?"

"That's a good question, and one that you should ask him. What would Scott say about you, I wonder? Would he tell me to trust you?"

"Well, I'm no longer planning on killing you, so that's a plus." I smiled. "I'll check in with Scott. If he thinks you're worth it, then you'll have nothing to worry about, at least not from me."

Just then, Eberhardt opened the door and walked in with coffee and muffins. He looked at the gun on the table and then at both of us.

I turned back to Richard. "Do you have a contact on the police force?"

"Of course I do." He walked briskly to his desk and reached for his transceiver. He placed a call but kept the vidscreen turned off. Instead, he gave a numerical code, which must have clearly identified him to the party on the other end, before he explained the reason for his call.

"What did I miss?" Eberhardt set breakfast on the table and picked up his gun.

I reached for a raspberry muffin and a cup of coffee, black. "It's Rose. We think she's working for Elaine Ramsey too."

"No shit! Really?"

I smiled and licked some crumbs off my fingers.

Richard rejoined us. "I underestimated her too," he said to Eberhardt. "The police will be here soon to investigate the robbery and death of Oren Johnson. We need to be out of here in half an hour." He turned to me. "You'll come with us?"

"No, I have to go to work, and so does Eberhardt."

Eberhardt nodded. "I'll stay and work with the police."

I looked at Richard. "Try to leave without being spotted, and let me go first. I'll be obvious and try to draw attention away from the building. If Mrs. Ramsey has hired anyone else, hopefully they'll follow me. I'll meet with her later this morning and tell her what happened to Oren."

I retrieved my coat and purse from the bedroom

and hurried to the front door. Before I reached it, Richard was at my side, his hand on my arm.

"Wait! Exactly what do you plan to tell her?"

I turned and gave him my full attention. "That I killed Oren Johnson. Don't worry, I won't tell her anything else."

"How can I reach you?"

"It's probably best that you don't, but if you need to, contact Scott."

I hurried through the hall, down the stairs and into the bright sunlight. Once on the street, I projected an air of confidence as I walked along, joining the flow of pedestrians and cyclists. Eventually, I paused and knocked on the window of a cab. It was a rusty old blue wagon. Hopefully, it would get me more than a few blocks before breaking down. I gave the driver directions to The String Bean, a restaurant a few blocks from my apartment.

I frequented The String Bean, since it was so close to home. Over time, the waitstaff and I had become friendly. Today, I walked in, chatted for a bit, and then exited through a side door. One could never be too cautious.

My apartment, located in one of Tkaron's nicer Working Class neighborhoods, could have easily fit into Richard's living room, but it was familiar and comfortable. It was home.

I kicked off my shoes and turned on an old techno musical device that had belonged to my mother. A woman's voice rang out clearly. "Just direct your feet...to the sunny side of the street..."

My mother had enjoyed music from the early 20th Century. The upbeat melodies and bright lyrics added color to our days. She'd told me that it masked the prevalent hardships of the time, hardships that seemed to be an ongoing experience for our people. I was drawn to the music because of the irony and because it reminded me of my mother.

I directed my feet past my bed and to my closet. The threadbare carpet was grey now. I had no idea what color it had been in its glory days.

Which outfit would work best for today? As always, I needed to look the part. I chose a pretty green dress speckled with tiny daisies. Shoes? White sandals. After a dab of lip color and something for my eyes, my look was complete, that of a lovely young saleswoman.

-Scott-
A Call from a Friend

My personal transceiver buzzed. "Maddock here."

"Hi, Scott!"

I recognized the voice, so I turned on the vidscreen for verification. "Rick! What's up?"

"We have a friend in common. Her name is Madeline."

How did they meet? In case anyone was tracking this call, I would keep it light, a conversation between friends. "Yes, Maddie! Wonderful girl."

"Beautiful too!"

"Sure is!"

"I understand you know her pretty well. What's your opinion of her?"

"She's loyal and trustworthy. She's a good find!"

"How much does she know about me?" Rick asked.

I shrugged. "We've never talked about you."

"You've known her for a long time, haven't you?"

I nodded.

"Well, have you ever, you know?"

If anyone was listening in, they would think we were talking about something else entirely, but I knew what Rick was really asking. He wanted to know how much I'd told Keira about the Resistance. The answer was, nothing.

"No. Circumstances were never right. And I guess I just wasn't sure how she would react. How long have you known her?"

"Not long, but it feels like we know each other pretty well already."

"Who made the first move, if I may ask?"

"She did."

So Keira had somehow learned about the Resistance, and she knew Guy was a contact. *What else does she know? Why did she contact him? Is she interested in joining, or does she need help?* Too little information could be dangerous. It was time to tell her.

"In my opinion, she's trustworthy but not trusting."

"Well, I thought a good start might be roses, but I don't know. Maybe it's too soon? Do you know what other flowers she likes — something more casual perhaps?"

"Flowers?" This wasn't about flowers. "I don't know, but I can find out for you."

"Thanks! I'd really like to make a connection, if you know what I mean."

I understood completely. Guy needed to get in touch with Keira, and it was important. I looked at the time. Those drills wouldn't run themselves.

"I have to go. But I'll talk with her soon and find out what kind of flowers she likes. Good luck!"

-Keira-
Double Crossed for Sure

It was still a little too early to leave, so I sat down in my shabby yet comfortable cranberry chair, leaned my head back and listened to some more music. "I've Got Rhythm" began to play. As the singer crooned about her man, a thought flitted through my head. Could Richard be "my man?" I chuckled. Could any man? Hardly. I knew it was better to be alone. Men were not to be trusted. The Elite were not to be trusted. The Gov was not to be trusted. Who was I kidding...most people were not to be trusted.

I reached toward the end table and picked up a small wooden box. Inside rested a shiny silver locket in the shape of a heart. I opened the locket and gazed at two tiny photos: my mother and my father, young, looking very much like April and Scott. From long ago, I remembered feelings of safety and happiness.

My father had given this locket to my mother shortly after they'd met. How did she know he was the man for her? What quality was it that allowed her to trust him with her heart and her life? *Family has to start somewhere.* Funny, I'd never thought about that before. I wished I'd had the chance to ask her about love. Did she really believe such a thing existed?

I believed in loyalty, not love. Loyalty was built through trust over time. That was real. What was love in comparison? Oh, I believed there was a biological connection between parents and their children. I'd felt a strong connection with my mother and father, but I was only eight when first my father and then my mother had...I closed my eyes and stopped the tears. There was no point dwelling on pain like that. I gently set the locket back in the box for safekeeping and stood up. It was time to go.

I approached Mrs. Ramsey's estate with a small pink suitcase in hand. The butler opened the door. He looked down his nose at me.

"Is the lady of the house available?" I politely inquired. He looked me up and down.

"May I ask who is calling?"

"My name is Miss Jones." I smiled. "You may tell the lady of the house that I have perfume to sample." I opened the suitcase and showed him my wares. He invited me into the front hall, then left to alert Mrs. Ramsey.

When she arrived, she led me into the sitting room and invited me to sit on an uncomfortable white chair. She rang a small silver bell. The maid immediately brought in a tray with two steaming cups of tea on saucers, a porcelain teapot and matching creamer and bowl of sugar cubes. The maid placed the tray on a low coffee table and slid the pocket doors closed behind her when she left.

"I was expecting money, not perfume," Mrs. Ramsey said as she lifted her teacup to her thin pale lips.

"You asked me to be discreet," I said.

"So I did," she replied with a chuckle. "Do you have my money? Is it hidden somewhere in that suitcase?"

"No. Unfortunately, it wasn't there." I added two cubes of sugar to my tea and took a sip.

"What do you mean, it wasn't there. Do you know where it is?" She smiled.

She was no good at this game. It was obvious she knew exactly where the money was.

"I mean it wasn't there. Mr. Johnson seemed genuinely surprised that it was missing."

"Of course he would react that way. Madeline, I'm disappointed in you. Sergeant Maddock recommended you highly, and after our first meeting, I expected more."

After Scott told me about this opportunity, I had followed Mrs. Ramsey and learned her routines. When her chauffeur picked her up one afternoon, I was already in the car. I had clearly surprised both of them with this maneuver. Elaine Ramsey had hired me on the spot and offered a large bounty for the completion of this particular job.

"Mr. Johnson accused me. He said I stole his money." I paused and took anther sip of tea. "I had to deal with the situation." I watched her closely. There was a sparkle in her eyes. She really did view other people's lives as a game. I would not disappoint her.

"What happened?" she inquired.

"I finished him, per your request. The story should be in tonight's news. Oren Johnson is dead, and nothing will be traced back to you. I'm sorry I was only able to complete half of the job." I placed my teacup in the saucer.

"Half a job of this magnitude deserves at least a quarter of the pay. I'll wire the gats to your account as soon as tonight's news verifies your information." She stood, obviously dismissing me.

Is that why she hired two of us? So she could weasel her way out of paying? "I must insist upon half, seeing as how I completed the more difficult and dangerous part of the job."

Mrs. Ramsey rang the silver bell, and her butler returned in time to hear her response. "Keira Maddock." She emphasized my real name. "You're lucky I'm offering a quarter. You see, you weren't able to find the money. You're lucky I'm planning to pay you anything, you ungrateful." She stopped herself, turned her head away and waved me toward the butler.

"Thank you, Mrs. Ramsey," I said, as I tilted my head in short bow. I picked up my suitcase and turned toward the door.

Apparently, she wasn't quite finished. "Keep in touch, Keira. I may require your services in the future."

This was seriously bad. It had been a test, and though I had passed, I had actually failed. I nodded but didn't look back.

On my way home, I located a public transceiver and called Scott. I needed to warn him. If Mrs. Ramsey knew who I was, she also knew that we were related. She could use that as leverage against him.

"Maddock here," he answered in his usual style.

I didn't identify myself and kept the vidscreen turned off. By doing so, he would know that this wasn't a social call from his sister. He would know to listen for clues.

"Scott, it's me. How are you? Have they been keeping you busy? I've missed you."

"I've missed you too. We really need to get together soon. We have a lot of catching up to do."

"Yes, we do! Life has been crazy lately." I was just about to tell him, somehow, that my cover had been blown when he interrupted, and I lost my train of thought.

"I can't wait to hear all about it. Does this have anything to do with a new man in your life?"

Richard must have already contacted him. It was true then, they really were friends, but why hadn't Scott ever mentioned him before?

"Yes, I was surprised to learn that you two knew each other," I said.

"We met a long time ago."

"Why didn't you tell me about him?"

"I'd rather discuss that in person."

Does Scott know that Richard is part of the Resistance? How much does he know about all of that anyway? The Resistance was a topic we'd never discussed. After all, Scott was military, and military personnel were loyal to the Gov. Scott only kept my secrets because I was family.

"He was hoping to impress you with roses. How would you feel about that?" Scott asked.

"That would be wonderful! I do love roses." I really didn't, and Scott knew that, but that didn't matter because this wasn't about flowers. What could Richard possibly have to tell me about Rose?

"Then it's too bad that he's decided against them. He seems to think it might scare you off if he gives you roses so early in the relationship." He paused. "Is this the beginning of a relationship?"

"Relationship?" I laughed. "Do you really think

I'm ready for a relationship with anyone?" Scott knew how I felt about love, but I had another question. "Do you think he's worth it?" *Will he understand what I'm really asking?*

He didn't hesitate. "Yes, I do. You can trust this Guy. He wants to know what other types of flowers you like. I think he wants to give them to you in person."

This Guy? He did understand, and he knew about Richard's ties to the Resistance. Apparently, Scott was willing to keep secrets for friends as well as family, or more likely, for close friends.

I looked down at my dress. "Daisies. You can tell him that I like daisies in the spring. I saw some beautiful flowers blooming in Liberty Park the other day." Now I sounded like April. "Scott, can you get away this afternoon?"

"Sorry, I'm heading out of town later today. I won't be back until the middle of next week."

"Then let's get together next weekend. It's important."

For the first time, I was glad I hadn't killed Richard. Scott never would have forgiven me for killing his good friend. He didn't approve of my line of work. He'd wanted me to join the military. By working as a Freelancer instead of a soldier, Scott worried that I'd be placing myself in "unscrupulous situations." I'd asked him if he even knew what unscrupulous meant because that's exactly why I wouldn't join the military. In my opinion, they were the Gov's lapdog.

-Keira-
What Happened to Rose?

A couple of hours later, I sat on a wooden bench in Liberty Park enjoying the sunshine when Eberhardt walked by. I stretched, stood up and followed far behind.

Eventually, he turned and entered an apartment complex in an Elite neighborhood, but I continued on. When I was sure I wasn't being followed, I made my way back. Eberhardt stood waiting just inside the front door. He led me down the hall and up the back stairs to an elegant two-bedroom apartment. Richard sat on a royal blue sofa in the living room, watching a newsvid. I settled into a matching chair while he paused the teleview embedded in the wall.

"Does this apartment have a whirlpool bath too?" I joked.

Richard ignored my question. "I was just checking the news. I'm dead."

Does he always have to be so serious? "Yes, as expected, but that's not why you contacted me. What's up with Rose?"

"She's dead too."

"What?" *Okay, this isn't the time for jokes.* Richard indicated the teleview, unpaused it and reversed the newsvid. Then he let it play from the beginning.

A typical announcer's voice spoke as footage of ambulances with flashing lights appeared on the screen. "In another tragedy, a hit and run caused the death of young Rose Brackaby, daughter of Minister Brackaby."

"Her father was in the Gov?" I mentally kicked myself for not knowing that.

"I thought you'd done your research."

I continued to watch the news as I replied, "Only on you. It can make my job more difficult if I know too many details."

"You mean if you begin to think about your targets as real people?"

What's he getting at? I tried to make eye contact, but he looked back at the teleview and avoided my gaze. "Was she important to you?"

"No." Richard laughed sadly and rested his head in his hands.

"What is it then? Do you think she would have joined the Resistance if Elaine Ramsey hadn't gotten to her?"

"I'd hoped so, but I'd recently decided it wasn't to be. Rose was involved in a number of committees and charities: Deliverance from Hunger, Keepers of the Children, Redemption for Orphans, but I'd come to realize that she was like so many of the others. It was all surface, a way to look good and feel good without actually doing good. When I first met her, I had hoped that by making a connection, together we could redirect resources from the wealthy to those who most need help."

"Are you Robin Hood or something?"

"Not exactly. My goal is to help others become more like Robin Hood. I try to cause a domino effect, people helping people by providing whatever they can, whether it's money or skills. Unfortunately, that wasn't Rose's goal, and now she's dead."

"You didn't cause her death," I assured him. "She has her own choices to blame for that."

Richard finally looked me in the eye. "Now she has no choices." He held my gaze. I was the first to look away.

-Guy-
A History

Keira looked away first. Was it a sign of remorse? I studied her. What was she thinking?

"What do you expect from me?" Keira finally blurted out. "Unless someone steps in, bad things happen to good people and good things happen to bad people. I've seen it over and over again. I try to change things, and I feel bad when people get caught in the crossfire, but I can't spend time worrying about it. It just happens sometimes. You can't let yourself get dragged down by that. Otherwise, you won't be any good to anyone."

Is this my chance? Can I convince her? "You have a strength, Keira, a strength I don't usually see in people. It's a strength of spirit. No wonder Scott trusts you."

"Scott trusts me? I was beginning to wonder," she replied sarcastically. "If he trusts me, why didn't he ever tell me about you?"

I decided not to answer her question, not yet. "Your anger adds to your strength, but it's misdirected. You can continue to take out 'the bad people,' or you can use your strengths to serve 'the good people.' If you choose the second, you can live, truly live, and stop simply surviving."

Could I help her? I wanted to, I really did. Scott had helped me to see clearly. I hoped I could finally return the favor.

"You asked how I knew Scott."

She nodded.

"We met when I transferred to your high school. We'd both been going through a rough time. My father had just uprooted me. That's how it had felt anyway. I was being relocated against my will. Scott was being relocated against his will too, but it wasn't the same. He'd been told he would have to leave in just a few months. He was preparing to move on."

"I remember. I was still at the junior high, but I remember how quiet and withdrawn Scott was at home. I was afraid he would leave, and we'd never see him again, or worse that we'd already lost him."

"I think most teenagers are selfish and self-centered. I was. Everything I wanted had always been provided, and until our move to Tkaron, I'd always gotten my way."

"You think Scott was being selfish?"

I shook my head. "Scott wasn't like anyone I'd ever met before. And he was never selfish. From what he told me, it sounded like he didn't expect anything to go his way. He worried that he was at the end of his life, not the beginning. Even so, even as everything he knew was ending, he put you first, you and your sister."

That was all I was willing to share with Keira for now. Would it be enough? Scott had changed my life. Would this conversation be enough to change hers? While she sat deep in thought, I remembered.

Scott and I had eaten lunch together every day for the rest of the school year. Our lunchtime conversations had allowed me to see the world from a different perspective.

That summer, Scott was hired to do yard work at a few wealthy estates. He was trying to earn as much money as he could to leave behind for his sisters. I began to work alongside him, but I refused payment, making sure Scott took 100% of the earnings. I didn't need the money – he did. I only wanted to experience what life was like for the majority of citizens who had to work hard to survive.

Later that summer, my father took me on a business trip to the Realm of Mediterra. We'd needed a special pass to be allowed inside their borders. My father had explained that most Mediterrans didn't like to do business with Terenians. We were fortunate that one of their corporations was willing to negotiate with our company. I saw possibilities in Mediterra that I'd never before imagined. If they could do all that, why couldn't we?

In just a few months, my views about life had changed completely. I'd decided that I wanted to devote my life to improving our realm. I began by using my family's influence and wealth to serve the less fortunate in any way I could. My father would have forbidden most of my actions. That only forced me to find creative ways to finance my projects. That was the start of it all, of everything that was important.

-Keira-
Crossroads

I thought about Richard's words. "You can live, truly live, and stop simply surviving." It was an invitation.

I'd had opportunities to join the Resistance before, but no one had ever given me a good reason to even consider it. Help people I didn't know? Why? No one had ever helped me or anyone I knew unless there was something in it for them. No, that wasn't entirely true. Richard had just reminded me that Scott had helped me and was always willing to help me. But that wasn't the same as helping strangers. I wondered, had Scott helped others, besides me and April? I sensed that my life had come to a crossroads, again.

The first time I'd been at a crossroads had been about a month before my sixteenth birthday. Scott and I had had a conversation in which he tried to convince me to join the military. He said I could easily pass the same tests he had.

I knew what he meant. He meant blood tests, genetic tests. I'd heard the rumors about Ramsey Corps and the military. It was common knowledge that a number of corporations dabbled in genetics, but some lines should never be crossed. I believed the rumors that said Ramsey Corps had crossed the line, and I didn't want any part of that! Every part of me belonged to me, and I wanted to keep it that way.

***

Late one night, we sat on the window seat in my bedroom. I stared at my reflection in the glass.

"I've heard the rumors. Can you tell me they aren't true?"

Scott was silent. I shifted my gaze to look at his reflection.

"Are you really all right with them taking parts of you, owning you in that way, after what they did to Mom and Dad?"

"Ramsey Corps is independent of the Gov," he insisted. "They didn't do anything to Mom and Dad."

During the last few wars, leaders of corporations that designed weaponry and scientists who dabbled in either germ warfare or genetic screening had become wealthy and powerful, the crème of the Elite. Toying with genetics had allowed germ warfare to reach new levels. It had been reported that our military could now target specific populations. And, genetic screening was the best way to determine which people could be trained and medicated to be the fastest, the strongest, the best. Because of genetic studies, Terene had won the last world war.

"Don't kid yourself, Scott. Ramsey Corps and others like it are the Gov. They created the Divide. You know as well as I that without the Divide, Mom and Dad would still be here."

"Keira, you need a job, a livelihood, and right

now, you have no training. You haven't even finished school."

"I'll finish. I just need to find a place to stay."

I'd been trying to figure out how I could survive yet keep my autonomy. Joining the military certainly would have been a means of survival, but it would have meant forfeiting my independence. I wasn't willing to do that.

***

Scott wasn't happy about it, but I'd made my decision. It had been a path of difficult times, cold times, hungry times and painful times, but I'd kept my independence. I'd also made a name for myself, and many throughout Tkaron respected and feared me.

What Richard was offering was different. He wasn't asking me to give up my independence. He was asking me to use my independence to help others.

He'd been waiting patiently, had given me plenty of time to think about his offer, but I still had some questions. "Why would I want to help people? Why do you?"

"Life shouldn't be like this, this Divide that we have in Terene. Ever since the war against Mediterra, our citizens have turned on each other, and many in the Gov have encouraged it. It benefits them. Don't you see? The workers outnumber the Gov and the heads of corporations, but rather than banding together and demanding a better life, they fight for the slim pickings they're given. This allows the Elite to keep all the money and power. It doesn't have to be like this, and it wasn't always so."

"Are you sure about that?" He sounded like Mom and Dad. "Are you sure it's not just wishful thinking?"

"I know it's not. I've seen..."

I wasn't done. "After all, there really aren't many jobs available, and most people barely have enough to get by. Even if the Elite were to share what they have, would there really be enough for everyone?"

"Keira, you said yourself, you see good things happening to bad people and bad things happening to good people. It doesn't have to be that way. It shouldn't be that way. You can help to change society for the better and make a living in the process."

"I'm already making a living, and I'm helping society get rid of some of the troublemakers. Our methods aren't even that different."

"Yes they are. You're only helping yourself, when you could be helping so many. You can change that."

"I can't change my outlook on the world just like that! Do you really think a person can just wake up one day and think, it's all going to be different from this moment forward?"

"I did, and Scott had a lot to do with that."

"Did he recommend that you join the military too?" I asked sarcastically.

"No," he replied seriously. "He wasn't even certain that it was his best option."

"Really? I thought that was always his plan."

"Maybe you don't know your brother as well as you think."

Does Richard know Scott better than I do? Does Scott share more with him than he does with me and April? I looked at Richard carefully and asked, "What has Scott told you?"

"I'm not certain I understand what you're

asking."

"What has Scott told you about me?"

"He said I can trust you."

"And?"

"And that you're independent, but I'd already guessed that."

I smiled, then asked, "Do you expect that good things will happen to you because you do good for others?"

"No, but I do believe the only way to heal our realm is to serve others. It doesn't really matter if "good things" come my way or not, but yes, it has worked out well for me."

I knew it!

Richard continued quietly. "You have an opportunity. What would your parents want you to do?"

I looked at him coldly. "What do you know about my parents? Just because Scott..."

He interrupted. "I'm sorry. Scott never talked about your parents. I only know that they're no longer with you."

"Oh." If Scott hadn't told him about that, then he couldn't possibly know Scott better than I did.

Both of our parents had died because of greed, and nobody had stepped in to help them. Where would I be now, what would I be like today, if people had been looking out for each other back then? Maybe Scott, April and I would have grown up happy.

As suddenly as it had come, my anger drained away. Only sadness remained. I was a product of my environment, doing to others what had been done to me. I was living a life of revenge. Could I change that? Did I even want to?

"I need some time to think." I stood. "Thank you for telling me what happened to Rose."

"Please, let Eberhardt drive you home."

"No thanks. I'll walk."

"Then let him walk you home."

Then they would know where I lived, and they'd know where to reach me. I guessed that would be all right. I nodded and looked at Eberhardt. He'd been so quiet I'd almost forgotten he was there.

We walked a few blocks in silence. Every once in a while a car drove by.

Eberhardt interrupted my thoughts. "Did Scott ever talk with you about the Resistance?"

"No, why would he?"

"He seems like a good candidate, doesn't he?"

I smiled, and then shook my head. "He's military. That's about as close as you can get without actually being the Gov! Do you know Scott too?"

"No, I've never met him. There are many reasons to join the Resistance, you know."

"Why did you join?" I asked.

"I'm not as noble as Guy, but I do respect him for that." Eberhardt paused. "I've been hurt." He traced his finger along the scar on his face. "People I love have been hurt and killed, and I want payback. The Resistance allows me to push back, hard." He grew quiet again.

We kept walking, lost in our own thoughts. I kicked some trash out of the way with my foot. It was another brochure touting the wrongdoings of the Gov.

"Why do you call him Guy?" I finally asked.

"It's not just a code name. It's the name he prefers, at least among those of us in the Resistance. He chose it for himself. You should ask him why."

"But I'm not part of the Resistance."

"You will be," Eberhardt concluded with certainty.

We walked the rest of the way in silence. As we neared my neighborhood, cars became virtually nonexistent. People lined the sidewalks, sat in the sun and enjoyed the bright sunny weather. Others walked along the street, heading this way or that. After a cold winter, the warmth was appreciated by all.

Richard and Eberhardt had both given me a lot to think about. *Can a few people really change society?*

-Keira-
Lunch with April

The next day, April and I met for lunch at a small café. We ordered bread and hummus to share. Meat that wasn't reserved for the military was either ultra expensive or unsafe.

"So, what have you been up to? The usual?" April combed her fingers through her long blond hair and pushed it out of her face. She had grown up to look so much like our mother.

"I've met someone." Had Scott ever told her about Rick?

"Really?" Her deep brown eyes brightened. "Do tell. Is he good looking?" She toyed with a pair of wedding bands that hung on a chain around her neck. They had belonged to our parents.

"Is that all it's ever about with you?"

"No, sometimes it's about money. Is he rich?"

"He's a friend of Scott's."

"Military," she assumed.

"No, from before."

"And they still keep in contact?"

"Apparently."

"What's his name?"

"Rick, well, Richard Burke the third."

"He sounds rich. How did you meet? Did Scott introduce you?"

"Not exactly. So...Scott never mentioned him?"

"No, I don't think so. Why?"

"No reason. We met at work."

"Oh no!" April rolled her eyes. "I hope he was an employer and not a mark. Either way, they say work relationships never last," she teased.

I smiled. "I've heard that before too. Plus, he's so different."

"What do you mean?"

"He's an idealist, like Mom and Dad, and...well, I'm not. I should just forget about it."

"Not so fast! They also say girls marry their father. No wonder you're attracted to him. Is he cute?" she asked again.

"Stop!" I playfully cuffed her alongside the face.

"Ow, hey, he is, isn't he?"

Just then, the Beckett's nanny arrived with two young girls in tow.

"Do you mind watching Edrea and Vanessa for a little while?" she asked April. "I need to run a personal errand."

April nodded. "Sure. We'll be in the park. Let's go, girls!" She motioned with her head for me to follow.

We settled down on the warm spring grass and watched the girls at play. They looked happy and innocent.

"Were we like that when we were young?" I asked.

"I don't know about you, but I am still young." April smiled and tossed her hair back.

"You know what I mean." I nudged her with my elbow.

"Yes, I do." She turned sober. "They're how I wish we could have been. We weren't given the opportunities they have."

I looked at her. Her life hadn't been easy either, though Scott and I had both supported her as much as possible.

"Do you think that's right? Do you think some children deserve that life and others don't?"

She shrugged. "It's just how things are."

"But, is it the way society has to be?"

"What's gotten into you, and what have you done with my sister?" April teased.

Rick's mood had rubbed off on me. I continued seriously, "It's not what Mom and Dad believed. Maybe Terene really was different once, more...I don't know, fair."

"I don't know that fair was ever an option, but if this guy is good looking and wealthy and into you, you could have the better life you're dreaming of, couldn't you?"

I wondered about that. Could Rick be into me? Oh, I knew I could make him like me – I'd seen the look in his eyes when he saw me in the bath. I was good at making men like me, but then it wouldn't be real.

On my way home, I stopped at my bank. When I tried to withdraw the money Mrs. Ramsey had promised to wire, the teller gave me a strange look and said, "I'm sorry, Miss. That account has been closed."

"What?" I asked in surprise.

"That account was closed," she repeated, "just this morning."

"By who?"

"I'm not a liberty to share that information."

"It's my account," I responded in a steely voice, "and you're telling me I don't have the right to know who closed it?"

I saw her gaze shift, and I glanced over my shoulder. She'd caught the eye of the security guard on duty.

I bit my tongue, then turned and walked calmly toward the exit. Suddenly, a guard reached for me. I dodged and ran out the door and into bright sunlight. A few blocks away, I hailed a cab. It didn't look like it would make it more than a few blocks, and the interior smelled funny. Nevertheless, I paid the driver and directed him to the Beckett estate. Upon arrival, I hurried around to the service entrance in back.

"Lewis." I nodded a greeting toward the chef. "Do you know where I can find April?"

"Hi, Keira. She's straightening the parlor for afternoon tea."

"Thank you." I hurried down the hall.

April had been living on site for over a year now, so I knew my way around. In the corridor, I passed the butler who also greeted me. I entered the parlor, walked over to the off-white fainting couch, pretended to faint and looked up at April.

"I need your help, sis."

"So dramatic!" She giggled. "I'll try my best. What do you need?"

"Information. Do you know of any upcoming social events in the next week or two? It's important."

"Why? You want to party?" She grinned, every bit the youngest.

"I'm serious about this."

April sat down next to me. "I can see that," she said quietly. "What's up?"

"She double crossed me and closed my bank account. Nobody does that to me and gets away with it!"

"Who? Wow, wait a minute." Her grin faded completely. "You're really angry."

"How can you tell?" I asked sarcastically.

"Other than the steam coming out of your ears? Look, go home and relax."

I looked at her like she'd gone insane.

"Really, I've got your back. Who did this to you?"

"Elaine Ramsey," I whispered. Her eyes grew wide, and I nodded to let her know how serious I was. "I need to know if she's throwing a party anytime soon."

"Cheer up! A lady of her standing throws parties all the time." April threw her arm around my shoulders. "They always talk about events like that during tea. That and who's engaged and whose wedding was horrendous and..." She stopped and gave me a look. "I'll eavesdrop this afternoon, and I'll stop by your apartment tonight."

"Thanks." I gave April a big hug. I didn't want to drag her into my affairs, but in this situation, it was the quickest way to get the information I needed.

***

Later that evening, April stopped by as promised. "I can't believe you pulled a job for Elaine Ramsey! Do you realize how influential she is? That's pretty risky, even for you."

"Well, she'd as much as told me she wasn't going to pay me, but I had no idea she'd close my account. Who steals from the Working Class anyway?"

"She does, obviously. But you'll get it back. She's

throwing a dinner party next Thursday at her Galt residence. You are just going to steal, right? I mean, you're not going to..." She slid a finger across her throat. "Not Elaine Ramsey."

I hugged her close. "Don't worry, April. I'll do what I do best. I'm a master of disguise. I'll sneak in and out. She won't even know I was there until it's too late. Then, I may have to disappear for a while, until she moves on and tries to take advantage of someone else."

I hated lying to April.

-Scott-
Meeting the President

I'd been in Parisio for a couple of days, preparing for my meeting. It was good to be back. I reached up to straighten my tie. Then I opened my briefcase, pulled out some documents and began paging through them, focusing on what I planned to say.

My associate chose a seat against the wall and waited patiently for the others to arrive. She didn't look it, but I knew that Madame Bellami was just as nervous as me. She had chosen to wear more colorful, yet dressy attire appropriate to her station. We both had high hopes that the Mediterran Gov would back our proposal.

"Monsieur President, messieurs, dames." I pushed back my chair and stood as the President and his advisors entered the meeting room. "I am truly honored that you've agreed to meet with me today."

"Shall we begin?" The President gestured to the chairs, and we all sat. "Let's get right down to business, shall we?"

"Yes, sir. Have you had a chance to read our proposal?"

"We have."

Some of his advisors nodded in agreement.

"You're a member of the Terenian military, are you not, M. Maddock?"

"I am, but you must understand that I am not here in that capacity, nor do I represent the Gov of Terene."

"You are a brave man, M. Maddock, to bring this proposal to our attention. Just by coming here today, you are placing yourself in danger. You understand that if we agree to this, you will likely be considered a traitor to your realm. Are you willing to sacrifice so much?"

"As long as there's a chance it will save others, yes."

"Are the rumors true?"

I hesitated.

"M. Maddock, are the rumors about genetic engineering true?"

I looked down as I thought about how best to answer his question. Rumors had been circulating for decades. Were they true? I just didn't know, but every so often a soldier would go missing. We'd been told they'd gone AWOL, that they had deserted, but I just didn't believe that. I'd known some of them personally. And all the tests they continued to give us, especially those of us in Special Ops...I raised my head and looked him in the eye. "I have no proof, but it's likely."

He nodded. "It is my understanding that you would only bring certain people into Mediterra, people who would be trained and then returned to help your cause."

"That's correct, as well as certain individuals who may require sanctuary. Obviously, there is no way to anticipate who would fall into that category. We plan to provide all funding."

"We must agree upon a cap. I will not allow undue strain upon the communities of Mediterra."

"Of course, if you'll turn to page 38, you'll see that we plan to be extremely selective. Our goal is to keep Terenian citizens safe within our own realm. However, we also recognize that it will not always be possible."

The President and his advisors took a moment to review page 38. Then he looked at me and asked, "Who is the other contact?"

"My partner, Guy Bensen. He has a better handle on the financial aspects, and I'm in charge of transport. We are equally invested in this opportunity. Our contact information is on page 5."

The President turned to page 5, reviewed the information, and then pushed the proposal away. He closed his eyes and thought for a few minutes.

Then he spoke, and everyone listened. "M. Maddock, I am impressed by your courage and by your selflessness. I did not expect that from a Terenian. You must know that the citizens of Mediterra generally make a practice of keeping to themselves. We do not want the problems created by others to become our own."

I nodded. We were not unaware that we had already achieved a victory just by being granted a meeting with the President.

"Because your organization is working to better your society, and based upon your character." He looked at each of his advisors in turn. All but one nodded. "We accept your proposal."

I let out a breath of air and smiled. "Thank you, M. President."

"There is one more matter to discuss before I make this official. This side venture. Explain it to me."

"I'm sure you realize, M. President, that illegal activities such as this occur on a daily basis in realms throughout the world. It's a lucrative way to fund our rescue operations. We want to make it legal on your end. We're offering the Mediterran Gov 15% from the sale of such items."

He paged through the proposal to that particular section. "And you are only agreeing to bring such items into the realm, not to export them without governmental authorization?"

"It's stated as such on page 56."

He turned to that page and suddenly looked up. "Who is Danielle Bellami?"

I smiled at her as she stood and moved forward. "M. President, I'd like to introduce you to Danielle Bellami, a highly respected Mediterran citizen and owner of Art Fantastique."

"Building bridges right from the beginning. I think your organization just may bring about the change you're hoping for." The President picked up a pen and signed the proposal in its entirety. "I wish you luck, M. Maddock, you and Guy Bensen. And you as well, Mme. Bellami."

The meeting had been a complete success – far better than we had dared to hope.

After the room cleared, I put my arms around Danielle and smiled at her. I leaned down until our foreheads touched. "How shall we celebrate?"

-Guy-
Can I Borrow the Car?

On Monday, Keira knocked on my front door just as I pocketed my transceiver and keys. She wore red exercise pants and a light jacket. Her hair was pulled back in a ponytail, and her forehead glistened with sweat. She flopped down on my sofa and grinned.

"I thought about all you've said, and I'm in."

"Now's not really a good time. Can you come back tonight?"

"This is important. I have business to discuss with you, but it shouldn't take long." She eyed my business suit. "How in the world did you find time to work undercover as Mrs. Ramsey's gardener and still make an appearance at your father's firm?"

"I have a somewhat flexible schedule. Are you certain this can't wait until evening?"

"Elaine Ramsey knows my real name, and she closed my bank account."

"Don't say another word." I pulled my transceiver from my pocket and placed a call to work, then turned so Keira wouldn't be in range of the vidscreen.

The image of Ellie, my secretary, appeared on the screen. "Mr. Burke, how may I help you?"

"If you would, please let the others know I'll be arriving late. They should begin the board meeting without me."

Ellie lowered her voice. "That's probably not the best idea. Your father is beginning to notice your absences."

I looked at Keira as I replied, "You know what's at stake. Do your best to cover for me. I'll be in as soon as possible."

I shut off the transceiver and gave Keira my full attention. "You're certain about Ramsey?"

"She called me by my real name and told me to keep in touch. She said she may need my services in the future, and my bank account was definitely closed. Security was even called when I asked for details."

"Has Elaine learned anything about the Resistance? Does she know Oren Johnson isn't really dead?"

She shook her head. "I don't think so. I think it's just me and Scott by default, but..."

"What is it?"

"Well, Scott already has to take orders from her because he's military...he said I can trust you."

"And you can."

She studied me for a minute, clearly worried. "I've been thinking about this all weekend, from every angle. I've been trying to figure out why. And I think Elaine Ramsey is tying up loose ends. We both know she hired me, and probably Rose, to get her money back, but I don't think she ever had any intention of paying either of us."

"What exactly are you saying, Keira?"

"The clerk wouldn't tell me who closed my account, but I think it's too much of a coincidence.

Elaine Ramsey must have closed it. She's the only one I can think of who has both the power and a motive to do that. I also suspect that she ordered a hit and run on Rose."

She paused and carefully monitored my expression. It was difficult, but I kept my gaze steady and gave no reaction. I wanted to hear it all.

Keira took a breath and continued, "Rose was a somebody, and she knew too much, so Ramsey had to remove her. Because Rose was Elite, Ramsey had to make certain that it looked like an accident. But Rick...I'm a nobody, plus she knows my real identity, so rather than kill me, she's sending a clear message that she's going to control me. I'm worried that closing my account is just the beginning."

"You're not a nobody. Do you need some money?"

"No." She shook her head vehemently. "I earn my own money."

Independent, Scott had said. He wasn't joking. "I can order false documentation if you need a new identity," I offered.

"No." She waved her hand. "I have connections for that too."

"Then how can I help?"

"I'd like to borrow your car and driver next Thursday."

I sat down next to her. "Why?"

"Mrs. Ramsey is throwing a dinner party at her Galt estate next Thursday. I need to be there."

"To do what exactly?"

"The party is my way in. I'll get the money back. Hopefully the amount you stole plus enough to make up for my closed account."

"So it's just about the money?" I didn't believe

she'd stop there, not when her cover had been compromised.

"I'll stick around," she confessed, "and after the party...that's when I'll do it."

I shook my head. "I think we should put someone else on the job, someone she won't suspect. We have people who are skilled at breaking and entering. They can get the money and send a strong warning."

I realized I was beginning to care for Keira, as Scott's sister and as an ally. And I wanted to protect her. Oh, I knew she could take care of herself, but killing takes its toll. I was beginning to worry about how Keira's choices would affect her, how they would impact who she would become.

"She'll suspect me no matter who you send in. I have to do this, or she'll own me. She knows too much, and she'll use that information to make me do whatever she wants. Anyway, you shouldn't risk someone else for me."

I sat quietly and tried to think of an alternative Keira might accept. "Let me send in Eberhardt as backup."

"No, I'll need him to drive, but I work alone. This is what I do. This is who I am. If you want me to work for your cause, don't ask me to change who I am."

I sighed. I couldn't change her mind this time, but maybe I could still help. "Be careful around her butler and chauffeur. They're trained bodyguards. The safe is in the master bedroom behind a Degas. The code is..."

"Behind a day-what?"

"Ballet dancers, painted by the artist Degas."

Keira stared at me blankly.

"You're not familiar with Edgar Degas?"

She shook her head. "What type of dancers?"

"Weren't you paying attention in school? What did you learn in your art and music classes?"

Keira gave me a strange look. "Working Class kids aren't allowed to take art or music classes past the third level, not unless they've already demonstrated talent."

"Really? Are you sure?"

"A friend of mine continued on as a painter, but that doesn't happen very often. I know nothing about art, and all I know about music I learned from my mother."

Even with as much as I'd learned since I'd met Scott, it was clear there were still gaps. I wondered if Keira would be willing to talk with me some more about her past, but now wasn't the time to ask.

"I'll take you to the theater and to a museum," I offered, "if you'd like. For now, I suggest that you take a moment to appreciate the painting before you remove it from the wall. I believe the one Mrs. Ramsey owns is an original."

"How do you know so much about her Galt residence? I thought you worked at her estate here in town."

"I was hired to landscape new garden arrangements at both, and I took some time to look around when she was out. I'll send Eberhardt over to pick you up next Thursday." I handed Keira a slip of paper on which I'd written down the code to the safe. "Here. There's a good chance she hasn't changed it since I didn't actually take anything from that estate. I wish you'd reconsider taking backup. I know someone who is skilled at breaking into high tech security. He would be invaluable if the code has been changed."

She reached for the piece of paper, and our fingers touched. "Thank you, but I'll be fine on my own."

-Keira-
Ramsey's Dinner Party

Thursday finally arrived. I dressed as part of the catering staff and wore the traditional short black skirt over black nylons and a pressed short-sleeved light blue shirt. I tucked my hair up under a blond wig. Although I didn't think she'd look too closely at the catering staff, I didn't want Mrs. Ramsey or her butler to recognize me while I was at the party.

As agreed, Eberhardt drove me to the town of Galt. Along the way, he described the layout of the mansion – more information, courtesy of Rick. The most difficult challenge would be climbing the main staircase in the front hall unnoticed. Eberhardt dropped me off a few blocks away from the estate.

As I walked along the main drive, I spotted Ramsey's chauffeur. I didn't slow my pace, and he didn't pay any attention to me as I walked around to the servants' entrance in back. I entered the kitchen and picked up a tray of hors d'oeuvres before anyone had the chance to notice that I didn't belong. As I walked through the kitchen toward the party, I palmed a paring knife and slipped it into a pocket of my skirt. I was ever watchful for Elaine Ramsey and her butler.

Some guests had already arrived. They chatted, drank and danced in the ballroom. Many wore military uniforms. Others had the look of Gov officials and other Elite.

I carried a platter of stuffed mushrooms as I made my way through the festive crowd. A few of the men patted my behind with one hand while choosing a mushroom with the other. I imagined Rick would say it was yet another way to keep the Divide strong – a way to degrade the Working Class and keep us in our place.

I noticed the main staircase through an ornate arched doorway and began to meander in that direction but stopped when I felt a hand on my shoulder. Startled, I turned. A man in uniform stared at me. His eyes were the exact same shade as mine, a perfect reflection of my own.

"Scott, what are you doing here?" I asked.

"I'm attending a party. You?"

"I'm working."

"Oh, no you don't."

"She didn't hold up her end of the bargain," I whispered.

"Keira," Scott said quietly as he shook his head. "I can't let you do this."

"Yes, you can, Scott. If you knew the whole truth, you'd let me."

Scott pulled me into a side room. No one noticed or cared. At parties like this, it was not uncommon for guests to sneak off with the help. Scott turned on a small lamp, leaned against the desk and folded his arms across his chest. I set down the tray and looked around. We were in a small library.

"You have five minutes. Convince me."

"Elaine Ramsey is not to be trusted," I began.

"Few are. Continue."

"She knows my real name. She knows we're related. You could be in danger too."

"I'm always in danger. Is that why you wanted to see me? Because of what she knows?"

I nodded.

"She's too influential, and you have other options. You should be avoiding her. You know how to disappear. It's time to take your losses with this one."

"No, that's not how it works. I can't disappear forever, and with the information she has, I'll have to do whatever she tells me to. And by threatening my safety, she'll control you too. I can't allow that!"

"You know better than that. She already controls me, to some degree. She's as close to the head-of-command any corporate leader can be."

"Wait, there's more. I'm sure you've been wondering how Rick and I met. Elaine Ramsey ordered a hit on him, only she didn't know him by that name." Now I had Scott's attention. "She hired me through you to kill one of your friends. Doesn't that bother you? Then she double-crossed me. That bothers me. Fortunately for all of us, things went wrong. I also called the other day because I wanted to talk with you about the Resistance but not here."

"No," he agreed, "not here and not tonight. Rick told you?"

I nodded again. "A little."

"Does Elaine know anything about that?"

"I don't think so, but Scott, Elaine Ramsey also murdered Rose Brackaby."

"Rose Brackaby died in a car accident."

"A planned accident."

Scott was pacing now, clearly agitated. "Are you

sure about all of this?"

"Absolutely," I lied.

"What's your plan?"

"To take her out, of course. She knows too much."

"Wait. Rick authorized that?"

"Authorized? Not exactly, but he knows I'm here."

"Just one minute." Scott pulled out his transceiver and placed a call. I noticed that he kept the vidscreen turned off and didn't use any names or mention specific places. Rick was likely doing the same on the other end. All Scott said was, "I'm here. What can you tell me about tonight?" He listened intently. "All right." He disconnected and looked at me. "Get back to work. I'll distract Ramsey."

"No Scott, I don't want you to get involved. I never wanted you to get involved in this." I shook my head sadly.

"Keira, I was already involved. Now do as I say."

I wrapped my arms around him and gave him a kiss on the cheek just as another guest entered with a pretty girl. Scott hurried back to the party, and I slipped down a side corridor. The front hall was mostly deserted, except for the butler who was relaxing in a chair now that most of the guests had arrived. My talk with Scott had taken too long. I waited patiently for a distraction. Soon enough, one of the kitchen staff brought over a plate of food. While they were talking, I began to climb the stairs with my head down. This wasn't the best opportunity, but unless another guest arrived, it was probably the best I would get.

"Hey!" I heard a voice call. Just then the doorbell rang. Damn, I should have waited, but how was I to know someone would arrive so late? I practically ran up the rest of the stairs, quickly located Elaine Ramsey's bedroom and turned on a small flashlight.

I'd modified this skirt with pockets in which to carry the tools of my trade. In addition to the flashlight and the knife I'd taken from the kitchen, I carried a thin black cloth bag and my black leather gloves. I pulled on the gloves.

Sorry, no time to enjoy the painting. With one quick glance, I decided that ballet costumes were whimsical but impractical. I wondered if this ballet type of dancing was meant to tell a fairy tale. I hadn't had much use for fairy tales in my life. I tossed the painting onto the bed and saw the door of the wall safe. This was a much more advanced model than I was used to. As quickly as possible, I entered the code. The safe didn't open. I punched the "clear" button and tried again. I didn't hear anyone yet, but I was certain the butler wouldn't be distracted for long. This time, the safe opened. I emptied the contents into my bag and turned off the flashlight.

As I crouched down, I pocketed the flashlight and pulled out the knife. Would I be able to take out the butler without the element of surprise on my side?

Quiet as a whisper, I moved toward the open bedroom door, slid behind it and set down the bag. A large shape moved into view and turned on the light. His gun was already drawn. He immediately saw the painting on the bed and the open wall safe and pushed against the door to ensure that no one was hiding behind it. I pushed back as hard as I could.

As the door slammed into the butler, I dropped down with as much force as I could muster and stabbed the knife through his foot. He stumbled. A grimace of pain crossed his face. Quickly, he regained his balance and pointed the gun directly at me.

I stood slowly, with my hands out to my sides, my gaze locked with his. I took a step backward.

"Stop!" he ordered. Just then I saw another shadow move behind him in the hall. I dove to the side. A muffled shot sounded, and the butler fell.

"Scott?" I called out. No, it was Eberhardt who reached out and helped me up. "Nice gloves," I said. They looked just like mine.

"Why did you call for Scott?" he asked.

"Not now. I should have known you wouldn't wait in the car."

"You're welcome. Let's go!"

"I haven't finished the job."

"And you won't tonight. With him dead, it's too hot. We need to get out now."

I sighed and then removed my gloves and shoved them into my pocket. I followed Eberhardt to the front staircase. Fortunately, luck was on our side, for the moment. No one was in the front hall, and no one seemed to have noticed that the butler was missing, yet.

Eberhardt pocketed his gloves and his gun. He pointed toward himself and then to the front door. Then he pointed at me and in the direction of the servants' entrance. I nodded. Eberhardt must have entered as a guest. I watched as he confidently strode into the night. Then I took a smaller side corridor to the servants' entrance and successfully bypassed the busy kitchen.

During the drive home, I had time to mull over the events of the evening. Rick shouldn't have sent in Eberhardt after I had specifically told him not to, but if he hadn't, I had to admit that I probably would have been captured or worse.

I silently studied Eberhardt.

After a few minutes, he turned in irritation. "What?"

"Thank you."

"It's what I do." He returned his attention to the road.

"Thank you just the same."

He glanced at me again. "Backup is a good thing, you know."

"Can I ask you something?"

"I guess."

"Where did you learn how?"

"How to what?"

"Let's see." I began to tick off items on my fingers. "How to infiltrate. How to take out a trained bodyguard without flinching. How to be backup."

"Oh, that." His eyes clouded over. "The military."

"Really? I didn't think people could leave."

"They can't."

"Rick?"

He looked at me. "Guy."

"When?"

"Not too long ago. I guess it's been about a year now."

"Did you fight in the last war?"

"The one against Mediterra?"

"Yes, the one that caused the Divide. Did you?"

"Yes."

A thought occurred to me. "Weren't you afraid you'd be recognized at Ramsey's party? There were a lot of soldiers there."

"I didn't mingle."

"Oh." Clearly, this conversation was over.

-Keira-
Scott Was There

When we arrived at Guy's apartment, he turned off the teleview and stood up.

"It's not over yet," I said as I set the bag of gats in the center of the dining table.

"What happened?"

"I got the money and Eberhardt took out the butler, but Ramsey is still alive."

Guy shot Eberhardt a concerned look.

"Had to." He shrugged. "She was cornered."

"I'll have to go back in a few days to finish the job. I won't be safe until she's gone."

"I still don't think you should."

"Obviously, or you would have told Eberhardt to wait in the car like we'd agreed."

Guy stared at me. "I never agreed to that. Let's talk about your other options."

"Scott talked about other options too. What did you say to him?"

"To help you."

I figured there was more Rick wasn't saying but decided not to press it.

"What does Scott have to do with this job?" Eberhardt asked.

"He was there, at the party," I said.

"What did he say to you?" Guy asked.

"He said, 'Don't do this,' until I told him she'd hired me to kill you."

Eberhardt looked at Guy. "Why was he at Ramsey's party? Did you send him in?"

"No, I already told you. He's military. He was invited to the party," I explained. "He's one of her soldiers."

Guy spoke so softly I almost missed what he said next. "Keira, Scott's one of us."

I pulled out a chair and sat down, completely deflated. I shook my head. "No, he would have told me. And he's military. Military is loyal to the Gov."

Guy knelt in front of me. "Keira, people are just people, no matter what their career or social standing may be. Many in the military swear loyalty to the Resistance, even above their loyalty to the Gov."

I looked at Guy accusingly. "You're not just a member of the Resistance. Not if you have the authority to send people in." I emphasized the last part.

He nodded. "You're right."

"But you didn't send Scott in tonight. He was surprised to see me."

"You'll find, Keira, that the first rule of the Resistance is secrecy. Secrecy is what keeps people safe. You'll be given information on a need to know basis only."

"That's why Scott never told me? Because you told him to keep it a secret?"

"You really should ask Scott about that."

"Not all secrets are good, you know. Just think, if you had told Scott about your plans at the Ramsey estate, he wouldn't have told me she was looking for someone to 'take care of a problem for her.'"

"He connected you two?"

"Yes."

Guy stood and quickly turned away so I couldn't see his expression, but I heard an intake of breath. Then he turned his attention to my black bag and dumped the gats onto the table. He formed three equal piles.

One pile he pushed toward Eberhardt. Guy looked him in the eye and said, "For your family."

Eberhardt nodded.

He pushed a second pile toward me. "Your payment for a job well done."

He then indicated the third pile. "For the Resistance."

I reached out and pushed most of my pile toward Guy. "I'll just keep enough for living expenses. Use the rest to help someone."

"You're certain?" He raised his eyebrows.

"Yes. I may not agree with you all the time, but like I said before, I'm in. I meant that," I assured him. "Guy?"

"Yes?"

"When we first met, you asked me if you could trust me. The answer is yes, you can."

"I believe you." He paused. "Keira..."

"Yes?"

"You can trust me too."

I got the feeling that Guy wanted to say more, so I waited for a minute. When he didn't continue, I said, "I'm tired." I turned my gaze to Eberhardt. "Would you mind driving me home?" We needed to talk.

-Guy-
Killing Is Never Good

I closed the door behind Keira and Eberhardt and went to the front window. Tonight went better than expected. I watched them walk to the car together. If anyone could convince her of the benefit of team operations, it would be him.

I was glad Keira had not killed Elaine Ramsey. Killing was never the best option. And Ramsey was too high profile. Removing her was too risky.

We would have to do something to make her lose interest in Keira though. Probably the best way would be to get Keira a new identity, whether she wanted one or not. If Keira Maddock couldn't be found, Elaine Ramsey would not be able to control her and could not use her as leverage against Scott.

Keira had also demonstrated her loyalty to the Resistance tonight, in more ways than I had anticipated. She was definitely an asset. Scott should have told her a long time ago.

I had to admit, I was starting to like her. Keira had a spark, an energy that I was drawn to. She forced me to think about situations from different perspectives, and she kept me on my toes. I smiled and turned away from the window.

-Keira-
My Apartment!

As Eberhardt pulled the car away from the curb and accelerated, I turned and glared at him. It was one thing to keep secrets, yet another to lie. "You told me you'd never met Scott," I accused. "Why?"

He raised his eyebrows in surprise. "I haven't met Scott."

"What? When you walked me home that day, you told me he wasn't part of the Resistance."

"No, I didn't."

"Well, you implied it. Do you keep secrets too?"

"It really is for the best. You don't need to know all the facts to follow orders."

"I don't follow orders. If I wanted to do that, I would have joined the military." I thought for a minute, and then said, "If you had met Scott before, you still wouldn't tell me. You would probably even lie to protect that secret, right?"

Eberhardt turned his head and gave me a steady look. "I haven't met him, but I know who he is. I've only ever seen him from a distance." He returned his attention to the road.

I sat back in my seat and mumbled under my breath, "I hate secrets," even though I knew very well that I had many of my own.

When we arrived in my neighborhood, the streets were nearly deserted, and it was very dark. Streetlights didn't work around here, so the unexpected light was almost blinding, and the noise left my ears ringing.

My heart jumped to my throat.

Eberhardt swerved to the side of the road and pulled to an abrupt stop.

My apartment! I pushed open the door and leaped out of the car. The sky was aglow. I pushed forward into the heat to witness the devastation that had been my apartment building.

My mother's locket, her music! I moaned and fell to my knees. My stomach reeled. Elaine Ramsey was still one step ahead of me. I stood and stumbled blindly to some low bushes. I threw up again and again, until there was nothing left.

Strong hands on my shoulders pulled me away from the bushes. Eberhardt turned me around until I was looking him in the eyes. He held my gaze until I was steady. Then he guided me back to the car. I collapsed onto the seat and bent forward with my head on my knees.

-Guy-
Bringing Her Back

I was just about ready for bed when I heard someone at the front door. No one other than Eberhardt and my parents had a key, and my parents would have called first. Did Eberhardt need to tell me something without Keira present, something that couldn't wait until morning? I hurried into the living room to see what he wanted but stopped short when I saw Keira. Eberhardt led her to the sofa. Her face was ashen.

"Her apartment just exploded," Eberhardt informed me.

"It burned down?" I asked, dumbfounded.

"No, it exploded," he repeated, "just as we arrived."

"Elaine Ramsey..." I began. "Could she have?" If there had been any doubt before, it was gone now. Keira was right. Elaine Ramsey had ordered a hit on Rose – there was no doubt about it. And this...this was more than a warning.

I sat down on the sofa and put my arm around Keira's shoulders. Eberhardt dropped into a nearby chair. Keira leaned into me and began to sob. Eventually, she settled and grew quiet.

"She's asleep," Eberhardt whispered.

"Thank you for bringing her back."

"Do you want me to stay?"

"No, you can go home. We'll talk tomorrow." He reached over and squeezed my shoulder.

I lifted Keira and carried her into the bedroom. She was so light and fragile-looking. One would never guess she was a Freelancer. I set her on the bed and gently removed her shoes. Then I sat down to watch over her.

Would this strengthen her resolve or weaken it? It was obvious that she'd been shaken to the core, but why exactly? Was it because of the attempt on her life? No, I felt it was something else. The building was just an apartment, wasn't it? I'd have to ask Scott exactly where they'd lived when their parents were still alive. Maybe the building itself had been important to her. Perhaps it was one her father had designed or maybe there was something important within her apartment. What had Keira lost tonight?

-Keira-
Needs

I woke when Guy set me gently on the bed, but I didn't open my eyes. *The locket, my mother's music, they're really gone. My last ties to my parents, gone.* I felt myself sinking. Breathing became difficult.

I was aware that Guy had not left the room – that he watched over me. After sinking and sinking and sinking some more, I realized I could no longer feel anything. I was just hollow, empty, gone. I needed to fill the void, to feel something other than the emptiness and the suffocating pressure on my chest.

I listened to Guy breathe: inhale – exhale – inhale – exhale. He sat next to me on the bed and held my hand. He kept me tethered to the world. I began to breathe in sync with him. It released some of the pressure. Scott said I could trust him. April suggested that I should seriously consider him. Even Guy had talked about trust.

I kept my eyes closed, pulled my hand away from his and reached out to caress his thigh. I willed him to lie down next to me, to gather me into his arms, to make me feel something.

When he didn't respond, I opened my eyes and

looked deeply into his. I wanted to sink into that sea of blue rather than into the blackness that surrounded me. I wanted to leave this world behind, if only for a little while. I stretched my hand toward his face and cupped his cheek, rough with stubble. Couldn't he understand what I needed? Didn't he want to help me?

He stood and backed away. I let my hand drop and just looked at him. *I'm wrong. He doesn't want me.* He turned and walked away.

-Guy-
A Decision

No, not like this. Not tonight and not as an act of desperation. I was shaking, but I refused to do something we would both regret.

I walked into the bathroom, closed the door behind me and leaned against it for support. When the shaking subsided, I walked over to the sink and turned on the faucet. The background noise helped me think. I leaned forward and gazed into the mirror until I'd made a decision.

I'll give Keira a place to stay for as long as she needs. Not here. One of the safe houses will be fine. I'll be there for her. We'll take it slow. She's loyal and trustworthy, Scott said. Maybe soon, I can trust her with more.

When I returned to the bedroom, she was already gone.

-Keira-
On the Run

Guy left. He shut me out. I sat up and pulled my knees under my chin. *What does he want from me? What does he expect?* I knew he wanted my help with the Resistance, so he must value my skills. He'd asked me all those questions, made me think about changing my ways. Didn't that mean he cared for me?

Who was I kidding? I didn't even believe in love. I was crazy to have thought he might want more.

It didn't matter. I could take care of myself. I was back in control. I had to be, and I knew I couldn't stay here. I needed to figure out my next move and get back on my own two feet. Where would I live now? I would have to pick up the pieces of my life and begin again. There, that was the answer. I would go back to the beginning and begin again.

My high heels swung at my side as I began a barefooted trek toward Tony's, a bar I knew well from my earliest days of living on the streets. Darkness sifted down from unlit streetlamps. When I spotted the familiar windows lit with candles, I hesitated. Did I really want to go down this path? I took a deep breath. Yes, right now I needed familiarity and a place to hide. Here, I knew what to expect, and I knew what would be expected of me.

I opened the door and made my way inside, into a roomful of people who had nowhere else to go. I scanned the crowd until I spotted him. Cole sat at a corner table, intent on some playing cards. A red pillar candle lit the players' faces. Cole wasn't the first person I'd stayed with back then. I'd met him a few months later.

I slipped behind him and gently placed my hands on his shoulders. The men across the table grinned in my direction, their poker chips momentarily forgotten. Greed reflected clearly in their eyes. As they looked me up and down, I became intensely aware of my short caterer's skirt. The women at the table regarded me with neither friendliness nor hostility.

Cole turned his head. "Ah Keira! It's been too long." He addressed the men. "Show some respect! Don't you know who this is?"

They looked confused.

"This is Keira Maddock. Tell me you've at least heard the stories?"

Two of the men looked down, but one shook his head. The woman on his right nudged him and pointed at a man seated at the bar. I looked too. How could I forget? He'd burned my left shoulder. He picked up his drink and took a sip.

"Hey, what happened to his fingers?" the man across from me asked.

Cole sighed and returned his attention to me. "I heard you were doing well for yourself." He looked at my outfit, and his eyebrows shot up. "I thought you were self employed though."

"I am. This was necessary for my last job. Cole, something's happened."

"Something that brought you to me?" He smiled.

"Did you see the fireworks display earlier this evening?"

"No, but I heard about it. You did that?"

"You know me better than that." I playfully slapped his arm. "That's not my style." I leaned down close to his ear and whispered, "Someone did that to me. I need a place to stay for a while, a place to lay low."

He set down his cards. "Did anyone follow you?"

"No, I'm pretty sure they think I was in the apartment."

"Chrissy's moving out." He glanced across the room and tilted his head in the direction of a petite brunette.

I turned to see Chrissy. With her was a tall slender woman I didn't recognize.

"She's moving up in the world. Payment includes room and board. How will you be paying this time?"

I needed to keep every gat I'd just earned. "In the usual way," I said.

Cole nodded in agreement and picked up his cards.

I walked over to Chrissy's table and looked for an empty chair.

"Oh, here," her friend said. "I was just leaving." She stood, then leaned down to give Chrissy a hug. "Congratulations!"

I sat in the vacated chair and ordered a beer.

"I saw you talking with Cole," Chrissy said.

"I need a place to stay. I hope you don't mind."

She shrugged. "I figured that's what you were talking about. I'll take the couch tonight."

"What's the good news?" I asked.

"I've replaced the Beckett's nanny."

"Oh? What happened to her?" My drink arrived, and I took a sip.

"Rumor is she's expecting, and Lance Beckett is the father."

I thought back to the other day when April and I had watched the Beckett girls at play in the park. Was that the errand the nanny needed to run?

"You be careful in that house. I wouldn't put it past him to try that again! Tell April to be careful too, won't you?"

"That's right! I saw her when I interviewed. I'll tell her."

"You've got an important job ahead of you now. You need to teach those girls to respect and appreciate the Working Class because one day they'll be at the top. We don't want them to end up like..." My thoughts drifted back to what Guy had said about people just being people, no matter what their station. "Well, like most of the Elite."

"That's a good point. Why are you back, Keira? Anything you want to talk about?"

"No, I'm not ready to talk about it just yet, but thanks for asking."

Chrissy nodded. "Anytime."

"You could help me out though. Would you pass along a message to April?"

"Of course!"

"You can tell her where I'm staying and that I'm okay, but remind her to be careful what she says to Scott."

"All right. Anything else?"

"No. Thanks, Chrissy."

"Sure. Are you about ready? I'm beat."

I tipped back my head and quickly downed the rest of the beer. Maybe the alcohol would help me get through the night.

Arm-in-arm, Chrissy and I walked the few blocks to Cole's house, a one-bedroom bungalow. I reached out and wiped a finger across the coffee table. Chrissy had cleaned. I sat down on the faded checkered couch in the living room and looked out the window at the night sky. Chrissy went into the bedroom to pack.

Now that I had a place to stay where I knew exactly what was expected of me, I could plan for the future. Tomorrow, I'd shop for some new clothes and purchase a few other necessities. Then I'd lay low for a few weeks. Once Elaine Ramsey believed she'd successfully killed me, I would be free to move on.

When Chrissy returned to the living room, I said goodnight, entered the small bedroom, removed my caterer's uniform in the dark and climbed into bed. I didn't want to dwell on what I'd lost so I surrendered myself to sleep.

Cole climbed into bed a couple of hours later. He caressed my shoulders and back until I was fully awake. It was time to pay the rent. I turned toward him and let him explore my body. I even reciprocated, but there was no emotion. This was, after all, just a business transaction. Afterward, I turned back to the wall and fell asleep.

-Keira-
Picking Up the Pieces

The next morning I climbed over Cole's sleeping form. Sunlight seeped around the edges of the old grey blanket that covered the bedroom window but streamed full force into the living room. I squinted in the sudden brilliance and noticed that Chrissy had already left.

I stumbled into the bathroom and splashed some water on my face. Cold. Jolted fully awake, I ran my fingers through my tangled mess of hair. Green eyes stared back at me from the wavy mirror. This was my world: cold, tangled and distorted. I shook my head. A previous boarder, maybe Chrissy, had left some perfumed soap. It helped make the cold shower bearable.

While I showered, I thought about recent events. When he'd realized who I was, Guy had said that Scott worried about me and wanted me to be safe and happy. I believed that was true. It sounded like my brother. For a little while, I'd thought maybe Guy wanted that for me too, and maybe he did. That didn't mean...a melody came to mind, and I sang a few lyrics:

But it wouldn't be make-believe,

If you believed in me.

Wake up, Keira. Guy made it clear. He wants a working relationship, nothing more. And I knew there was absolutely nothing wrong with that, but it still hurt. We had talked about trust, not love. I'd never before believed in love anyway, so nothing had really changed. The locket being destroyed the same night that Guy pushed me away, well that was just a stinking coincidence.

Scott trusted him, and Guy could trust me. I would never betray him or the Resistance. That truth remained. I felt that in a couple of weeks, I'd be able to move past these new emotions and approach him about another job. I could still pick up bounties on the side. I could do both, take out the Bad and help the Good.

I turned off the water, wrapped myself in a thin light blue towel and returned to the darkness of the bedroom. I rummaged around in Cole's closet until I found a clean pair of jeans and a plain black T-shirt. Both were too big, so I tightened the jeans with a belt and rolled the cuffs. Then I tucked in the shirt and put on my heels. Back in the living room, I picked up an old baseball cap I'd seen the night before. I twisted up my hair and tucked it under the cap.

My stomach grumbled so I hurried to the kitchen and opened the refrigerator. I could tell the electricity had been off for at least a couple of hours. Inside was a six-pack of warm beer, a half stick of butter, some outdated eggs and half a loaf of bread. I tossed out the eggs and settled my stomach with a slice of bread and butter.

The golden sun and bright blue sky lifted my spirits. I had nowhere pressing to be, and I wouldn't be able to look for work for a little while. I needed to lay low to give Elaine Ramsey time to believe she had accomplished her goal. Certainly, people had died in that explosion. Let Mrs. Ramsey believe one of the corpses was mine. The Gov wouldn't spend too much time identifying the bodies, or what was left of them, not in that part of town.

At a second hand clothing store, I found a couple pairs of fitted jeans, black and dark blue, and a few stylish tops to wear with them. I also purchased a light spring jacket, a pair of comfortable sandals and a trendy black pack in which to carry my items while I was living on the run.

Next, I stopped by a drugstore and bought some personal items to add to my pack as well as a pair of scissors. In a public restroom, I cut my long hair short. I'd ask April to fix the back when I next saw her. Then I put on my new shoes and shoved my high heels into the pack with the rest of my belongings.

I saved my few remaining gats and began the long walk back to Cole's.

-Guy-
A Meeting with Scott

Board meetings, lunch meetings, endless meetings! Pushing gats this way and that, back and forth among the rich – never in the right direction. That was all life at the firm ever was and ever would be.

Before I'd always had the Resistance to give balance and meaning to my life. Now, only two thoughts kept running through my mind. One was Elaine Ramsey. Was she still a threat? And what about Keira? Where was she? Was she safe?

The morning after she left, I instructed Eberhardt to drive around the city searching for her. After four days with no leads, I called Scott to arrange a lunch meeting. Our cover, as usual, was to discuss his portfolio.

"Hello, how have you been?" I placed a cloth napkin on my lap. Scott sat opposite me in a fancy restaurant just off the base.

"I've been better. You?" His voice was like ice. I'd never heard him sound quite like that before.

"I've been better too," I confided. A waitress arrived to take our orders. As soon as she left, I said, "Keira is missing, and I'm worried sick."

"She's not with you then?"

Was that why he was angry with me? Because he thought she was with me, and I hadn't told him?

"No, she's not."

"And you don't know where she is." It wasn't a question.

"No, I don't."

"So that's why you didn't call." His voice had a warmer tone now. "But, you do know what happened to her apartment, right?"

"Yes, I know, but she wasn't there when it...happened. You don't know where she is either?"

"She doesn't want to be found, but I'll be seeing her in a couple of days."

"You've been in contact with her! Is she all right?"

"I didn't say that. I haven't spoken with her yet. She's playing this her way. I'm surprised she didn't go to you though. If there was ever a time for her to turn to the Resistance for help, this was it!"

I dropped my gaze, too ashamed to tell him what had really happened.

"What is it?"

"She came to me, but I pushed her away. It wasn't my intention," I quickly added. If I hadn't walked out of the bedroom that night...if I had instead...she definitely would have stayed. "Do you think I can convince her to come back?"

"I'll talk with her, but I can't promise anything."

We sat quietly, lost in thought, until our food arrived.

After a few bites, Scott looked at me and said, "How do you feel about her?"

I looked right back. "Isn't it obvious?" I heard the intake of his breath.

"I have an idea, something that may help."

"What do you have in mind?" I asked.

"I'll encourage Keira to see you, and I have something I'd like you to give her. But if she decides not to see you, I'll want it back." He reached into his bag and retrieved a thin book. "This belonged to our father. It's a book of poetry. It was a gift from our mother. Each of us took something to remember them by. The locket Keira had and some musical recordings that our mother loved...well, she always kept them safe in her apartment. Anyway, I'd like for her to have this book. I think she may need it more than I do right now."

"You could give it to her yourself."

"That was the plan, but I think it may mean more coming from you." He handed me the book, and I gratefully accepted it.

"I have something else." He reached into his pocket and took out a slip of paper with an address on it and a key. "I have a week on holiday coming up. I was going to go with...a friend, but I'd rather you took Keira there instead, if she'll let you. She's never been on holiday." He tried to hand me the address and key, but I waved them away.

"Well, then it's about time, but you should keep your week on holiday. I can afford to take Keira anywhere she'd like to go."

"I know you can, but I insist that you take her here." Again he held out the key and address. "We're partners, aren't we? Equals?"

"We always have been," I assured him as I accepted his gift. "Thank you."

When I climbed into the car a half hour later, Eberhardt asked, "Did we find her?"

"No, but Scott said she's all right." Then I

hesitated. Scott hadn't said that. He just said he would be seeing her. He didn't even know where she was. Where could she have gone? Not to Scott, obviously. Was she with her sister? I realized I didn't even know her sister's name. Probably not, Scott would have known if she was with family.

More than once, Scott had described Keira as independent. I tried to think like her. What would she do now, after her most valuable possessions had been destroyed?

Eberhardt immediately noticed my expression in the rear view mirror. "What's wrong?"

"I think she may be planning to take out Elaine Ramsey by herself, whatever the cost."

"That's no surprise," he said. "It's what I would do."

I looked at him in alarm.

He looked back. "She hasn't done anything yet."

-Scott-
Liberty Park

Several days ago, I heard a news report about an explosion at an apartment complex. They attributed it to outdated electrical wiring – 53 dead. I watched the reflection of the teleview in the mirror and set down my razor. I recognized that neighborhood and immediately called April. She hadn't heard anything. We were both worried but refused to accept the worst.

I'd last seen Keira at Ramsey's party. When I'd left, Elaine Ramsey was still saying goodbye to her departing guests, and Keira was nowhere in sight. I had a feeling she was hiding somewhere in the house waiting for an opportunity. And the next morning, I saw the news.

Later that day, I received a call. "Maddock here." I turned on the vidscreen.

April's image appeared, her brow furrowed. "Can we get together sometime soon? I'm so worried about Keira."

She didn't sound quite like herself. Keira must have contacted her somehow. "I'll be done at noon on Wednesday. Where?"

"By the trees."

"I'll be there."

***

April and Keira sat on a blanket in front of the apple trees. They stood as I approached. Keira had cut her hair; short dark curls framed her face. I leaned down to hug them both.

"You're late," Keira said. "Is everything okay?"

"I was followed, had to shake him. Where are you staying?"

"With Cole."

"I'll kill him."

"No, you won't," she said firmly. "This was my choice, Scott. I went to him. Cole's done nothing wrong, and he treats me way better than most."

"That doesn't make him a good person. Has he hurt you?"

"No! He never has. See, no scratches or bruises." She stood up and spun around. "No new ones anyway."

"Well, that's a start. You do know what he is, what he does? He's very well known in certain circles."

"I don't partake. Besides he only sells to the Elite and the..." She looked at me then with a question in her eyes. "You don't, do you Scott?"

"No, I don't do drugs," I responded emphatically, even though that wasn't entirely true. Every soldier in Special Ops was expected to take certain drugs to enhance performance in the line of duty. "It's likely he's killed, you know. In his line of work..."

"And I'm a Freelancer. What do you think I do?" she countered.

"Cole doesn't love you."

"Nobody said he did. He's just giving me a place to stay." April leaned over and gave her a hug.

"Really? Is he helping a friend in need, or is he charging you?"

Keira looked away, so it was as I'd assumed.

"His price is fair," she responded quietly, "and he honestly hasn't hurt me."

"I could give you money."

"No, I take care of myself. You know that Scott." Yes, I knew. Keira had never accepted money from me, not even when I'd worked so hard just for them. At least April had accepted my help back then, and I knew she made sure some of that money had benefited Keira too.

"Keira..." I sighed and shook my head. I wished she'd let me help her, but I had to be careful. If I said the wrong thing, she may run again. To complicate matters, we couldn't speak freely in front of April. As far as I knew, she didn't know anything at all about the Resistance. "I've spoken with Rick."

"What's he like?" April asked.

"Worth it," I said to Keira. "I think he has real feelings for you."

"No." She shook her head, and her eyes grew dark. "I went to him first. He turned me down."

"Oh Keira!" said April. "That could be a good sign."

"How would you know?" she spat.

"Well, I've met someone." April sounded hurt.

Keira and I both looked at her in surprise.

"It's the new groundskeeper." April blushed.

"What's he like?" Keira asked.

"Oh no! No distractions. Today we're talking about you, not me."

I returned my attention to Keira. "I think you

should see him, at least one more time." I paused. "There is something else I wanted to discuss with you."

"What is it?"

"Have you been paying attention to the news?"

"Not much electricity where I'm staying," she pointed out, "so no."

"There was a...well an attack at the Ramsey estate."

"Oh yeah, the butler..."

"Not the butler. The chauffeur."

She looked convincingly shocked.

"You didn't know?" I asked, my eyebrows raised.

"What are you implying, Scott? No, I didn't know. I'm not the one keeping secrets," she accused quietly.

I held her gaze but didn't speak. April looked back and forth between us but didn't say anything.

"How?" Keira finally asked. "What happened?"

"It was a car bomb. Her chauffeur was killed instantly. It happened a couple of days ago."

"Her chauffeur? You mean her bodyguard."

"Yes, it was clearly retaliation for what she did to you. Don't you think?"

-April-
Ashton

When I arrived at the park, Keira was already there, on a bench in the shade. She smiled and stood as I approached.

"Would you like to stay in the shade or enjoy some sun?" I held up the blanket I'd brought along.

"Enjoying some sun sounds perfect." She smiled at me and took one end of the blanket. We spread it on a grassy knoll.

"You've cut your hair."

"Will you help me even it out?" She handed me the scissors.

"Are you going to dye it too?" I asked.

"Maybe."

"Would you go back to red?"

"No, not yet. Maybe I'll try your color."

I smiled. "That would be nice. Then we might actually look like sisters."

We sat down together and faced the three apple trees we used to climb when we were children. I went to work on her hair. The birds twittered in the trees, and the sun warmed my bare arms. I breathed in deeply and felt the muscles in my shoulders begin to relax.

"Are you all right, Keira? I mean really all right?" I'd been able to help her in the past. Did she need my help again? "Remember the first time you stayed with Cole? I was so worried."

"I wasn't with Cole back then. It took me a long time to figure out who was safe." Keira turned and gave me a reassuring hug. "I'm safe with Cole. Haven't I always let you know where I'm staying, and how you can reach me?"

"Ever since those first few weeks, yes." She was right. She had. "If you need a place to stay though, I could sneak you in. Here, I'm finished." I handed her the scissors.

"And jeopardize your job? That's not a good idea, April."

Losing my job might not be so bad, but she was right to worry, then we'd both be on the street. How would we survive? I didn't have any savings of which to speak. Live in help received payment mostly in the form of room and board, and Keira's accounts had been closed.

Just then we saw Scott. I wondered if he could loan Keira some money, but quickly dismissed the idea. I knew that Keira would never accept. We stood and each received a warm hug from our big brother. Then we sat again, the three of us together, like old times.

Our parents used to bring us to this park. The apple trees were much smaller then. They had grown and twisted with age. I thought about how similar we were to those trees: beauty on the outside masked a twisted and shady interior. Well, the trees reminded me of Keira and me actually. Scott had been luckier; he'd had more opportunities.

"Where are you staying?" Scott asked Keira.

I watched the rest of their exchange with interest. Scott really didn't like Cole.

"Has he hurt you?" he asked.

"No! He never has. See, no scratches or bruises." She stood up and spun around. "No new ones anyway."

We both knew she'd been hurt before, but I trusted that Keira was telling the truth about Cole. I'd stayed with him before too, but Keira didn't need to know about that. While I'd been lost in thought, their conversation had continued.

"I've spoken with Rick," Scott said.

Now that was an interesting topic! "What's he like?" I asked.

"Worth it," Scott said and turned back to Keira. "I think he has real feelings for you."

"No," she said, and her eyes grew dark. "I went to him first. He turned me down."

"Oh, Keira! That could be a good sign."

"How would you know?" she asked harshly.

That hurt! She didn't think I knew much, but I knew a lot more than she realized. She didn't know that I protected her too. "Well, I've met someone," I revealed.

Keira and Scott both looked at me. I read the surprise in their eyes. Was it really such shocking news?

"It's the new groundskeeper." A warm glow rushed to my cheeks.

"What's he like?" Keira asked.

"Oh no, no distractions. Today we're talking about you, not me." Today our focus should be Keira. Besides, I wasn't ready to share details just yet.

"I think you should see him," Scott reiterated. He

meant his friend, Rick. "At least one more time." He paused to let her think it over. Then he shared something really important about an attack at the Ramsey estate. He said it was in the news. Keira looked shocked. "You didn't know?" he asked her.

"What are you implying, Scott? No, I didn't know. I'm not the one keeping secrets." She gave him such a cold look. I shivered.

What's this? Keira accusing Scott? What secrets has she uncovered about him? I knew what she'd do if she ever learned my darkest secrets, and I didn't want her to kill for me. That's why she mustn't ever find out.

A short while later, after a walk around the park together, I had to leave. When Keira gave me one last hug, she whispered in my ear, "I'm sorry. You don't deserve my anger. You and I are going to have a talk one day very soon about this new groundskeeper."

I smiled as I waved goodbye. Then I hurried back to the Beckett estate to resume my duties and to see Ashton again. Well, to watch him from a distance actually. Scott and Keira didn't need to know that so far, this was only a crush. I was sure Ashton would notice me soon enough. Most of the male servants did because of the uniform Mr. Beckett required me to wear – a very short black skirt and a tight white blouse.

It was my understanding that a maid's job was to keep people happy. We kept the mistress of the house happy by keeping the environment clean and organized and by running any errands she didn't want to do herself. We kept the master of the house happy in other ways.

I was pretty sure that everyone involved was well

aware of this arrangement. As long as we were discreet, everyone saved face and everyone, except me, remained happy. When I was hired, I knew what would be expected of me. I could see it in Lance Beckett's expression, by the way his eyes roved over my body during the interview.

So why had I accepted the position? It was a job, and there weren't many of those available in Tkaron. I couldn't continue to rely on Keira forever. I needed a way to support myself. Anyway, people with no money were ruled by those who had money. It was that way throughout the entire realm, especially since the end of the last war. As for the rest of the world? I knew Terene fared better than most. According to the adspace and billboards, we were very lucky. As a whole, Terene continued to prosper.

Even so, I was always on the lookout for opportunities to improve my situation. And now, something wonderful had happened! Being in the right place at the right time had brought Ashton into my life. He wasn't wealthy, but he was hard working and self-sufficient. It didn't hurt that he was good looking too. I sensed a positive change in my future.

When I returned to the estate, I spotted Ashton alone in the garden. This was my chance!

"Hello and welcome!" I said as I ventured off the cobblestone path. I offered him my hand.

Ashton wiped some dirt on his slacks, took my right hand in his and covered it with his left in a warm handshake. He was not wearing a ring.

I smiled. "I'm April. It's nice to finally meet you!"

"Are you one of the family?"

"No, the maid. Only I'm not in uniform because I was away on personal business during my lunch break."

He looked at the level of the sun. "Lunch break? Do you normally take such a late lunch?"

"No, not usually, but like I said, I had some personal business, so Mrs. Beckett authorized a later lunch time for me today. I've been here long enough, to be granted such privileges. Mrs. Beckett is fair, you'll see."

"What about Mr. Beckett?"

I avoided the question. "Even with the later lunch time, I'm sure I'll be missed in the house if I don't return immediately. I hope we'll have the chance to talk again soon." I smiled nervously and backed away. Then I turned and walked around to the servants' entrance. I couldn't believe what I'd implied about Mr. Beckett. If I were caught saying the wrong things about my employers, I could lose my position.

I looked down at my hand and smiled. It was still warm from Ashton's touch.

-Keira-
Dinner at Tony's

After April left the park, Scott and I had some time to talk privately. I shot him a dark look.

"I'm sorry, Keira," he began. "I should have told you, maybe not right away, but long before now. Just before your sixteenth birthday...that would have been a good time. Maybe I could have convinced you to join the military by telling you about the Resistance."

"The two don't exactly seem to go hand-in-hand."

"That's why it's a perfect cover! Don't you see? Nobody in the Gov expects military to be working for the Resistance."

"So, is everyone in the military initiated? Is that how you learned about it?"

"Initiated? No! Not all soldiers are part of it, but many are."

"How did you get involved?"

"Through Rick," he paused. "Keira, he can help you. Don't give me that look! You don't even have to be part of the Resistance if you don't want to. Rick will help you no matter what. He cares about you. Please, just call him."

***

Later that day, I returned to Tony's for dinner. I found an empty booth and ordered the daily special. It was the best value, and other than an occasional beer, it was all Cole would allow his boarders to order on his tab.

While I waited for my food to arrive, I thought about what Scott had said. *Could I have been wrong about Rick? Does he have feelings for me? Could he even love me? What does that even mean?* I'd never known anyone besides Scott and April who meant anything to me before.

Rick was the opposite, I realized. He seemed to believe that most people were important, that life was important. Maybe that's why he became a leader in the Resistance.

But Scott seemed to think that Rick cared for me specifically. Did he? Then why had he walked away? *Could I ever be more important to him than the Resistance was? Could the Resistance become as important to me as it was to him?*

Cole spotted me across the bar, sauntered over and sidled into the other seat. My food arrived, and he placed an order for himself. He studied me for a minute while I picked at my food.

"You're thinking again. You've been doing that a lot lately. I've seen you dark and gloomy before, but this time it's different."

"I've had a lot on my mind."

"When you arrived, you told me this was temporary, until you could get back on your feet."

"Yes, do you want me to leave?"

"Want you to leave? Nah...but someone else has

117

expressed an interest in boarding. You can both stay. It could be fun." He winked.

"I'll pass. I'll take the sofa and try to be out in a day or two."

"All right, but if you stay past the weekend, I'll have to insist on another week's rent, even if you're not into that."

I nodded. I'd be gone before then. "Cole?"

"Yeah?"

"You've never hurt me."

He raised an eyebrow. "I thought you weren't into that either."

"I'm not, but what makes you different than the rest of the men around here?" I nodded my head toward the bar.

"Can you keep a secret?"

I rolled my eyes, more secrets!

"Image."

"What?"

"It's all about image. People around here, they know what you're like. They tread carefully for fear of losing, appendages. Having you around helps my image, and I know that you're more likely to come around if I don't hurt you. It also keeps me in possession of all of my...appendages." He smiled. "You get what you need, a safe place to stay, and I get what I need, image."

"Oh." I looked away. It was like I thought. People didn't give without receiving something substantial in return, and apparently, Cole was receiving a lot more than just the rent.

"Well, it's been...quiet, having you around this time. It's been a nice change in my routine." He sounded sincere. His food arrived, and we ate in comfortable silence.

I continued to think about the latest news. Scott said there had been an attack at the Ramsey estate. Had Rick ordered a hit? Had he meant to kill her? Even from the little I knew about him, it seemed unlikely. Now Eberhardt...bombs and guns were his style. Had he taken it upon himself to do what he knew his boss wouldn't condone? But why? Especially after I'd accused him of lying to me. What would either of them gain? It was time to find out.

I smiled at Cole and stood, then walked over to a public transceiver in the back corner and entered Guy's number. I turned on the vidscreen.

"Keira! How are you?" He sounded concerned.

"I'm fine. I can take care of myself."

"I have no doubt about that. May I see you?"

"Yes," I said quietly. "Where?"

"Would you meet me for dinner at the Café de Rivoli tomorrow at 6:00?"

I smiled at his choice of restaurants. "I'll be there."

-Guy-
The Road Less Traveled

I stood when I noticed Keira walking toward my table. I almost didn't recognize her. Short curly blond hair framed her face and dark blue jeans enhanced her curves. A lacy green shirt caused her emerald eyes to sparkle.

"Hello, I'm Guy Bensen, and you are?"

"Keira Maddock. It's a pleasure to meet you." She held out her hand.

Instead of a handshake, I gently pressed my lips to the back of her hand. I looked up to see a genuine smile. I pulled out her chair, and Keira placed a black pack at her feet as she sat down.

The waiter arrived, and I ordered drinks, imported Chardonnay.

I leaned forward and spoke quietly. "Thank you for agreeing to see me."

She nodded and responded just as quietly. "Thank you for inviting me to dinner...Elaine Ramsey, that was you?"

My smile disappeared. "Eberhardt. I wish he hadn't done that. It's not like him to take matters into his own hands. He usually follows orders. It does complicate things."

She nodded. "I know. If she thought I was dead, she doesn't anymore. Even Scott thought the bomb was my doing. It's why I dyed my hair." She reached up to toy with a few curls.

"You should change your name."

She shook her head. "Not yet. I don't have a bank account anymore. My apartment is gone. Madeline Jones is gone. All my paperwork on her was in my apartment when...anyway, as long as I continue to lay low, Ramsey shouldn't be able to track me."

I nodded. I wouldn't bring it up again, but I would get the process started, just in case.

The waiter returned with our drinks, and I placed identical orders: the house salad, tilapia and steamed vegetables.

When he left, I noticed a question in Keira's eyes.

"Why did you want to see me?" she asked.

I picked up a thin book, opened it and began to recite:

> Two roads diverged in a yellow wood,
> And sorry I could not travel both
> And be one traveler, long I stood
> And looked down one as far as I could
> To where it bent in the undergrowth;
> Then took the other, as just as fair...

Keira concluded the poem:

> Two roads diverged in a wood, and I-
> I took the one less traveled by,
> And that has made all the difference.

"The Road Not Taken, by Robert Frost. Where did you get that?"

I handed her the book. "It was your father's. Scott wanted you to have it. That poem means a lot to me too. I've never been one to take the popular route." I hesitated, but only for a moment. "I hope I haven't missed the right road," I finished in a rush.

She smiled. "But how can we know which is the right road?"

"I think I know." I looked directly into her radiant eyes. She held my gaze.

Our food arrived then. I looked away and took a deep breath.

During dinner, we talked about our childhoods. They had been different, to say the least.

Afterward, I asked, "Do you have anywhere you need to be tonight?"

"No, nowhere."

"Will you walk with me? It's such a beautiful evening."

"All right."

"May I carry that for you?" I indicated the black pack into which she'd placed the book of poetry. I wondered what else was in it. It probably contained everything she owned.

"I can carry it myself." She spoke quickly but then looked at me and appeared to have second thoughts. "Um...okay." She handed me the pack. "Thank you."

The setting sun cast a pink hue on the horizon. As we walked, I gently took her hand in mine. Keira didn't pull away so I laced my fingers through hers. We continued on, enjoying each others' company.

"Hey, I know where we are." She stopped suddenly and looked up at a tall apartment complex. "Didn't a man named Oren Johnson used to live here?"

"Yes, he was renting from me, but I haven't heard from him in some time," I teased. "I think he skipped out on the rent."

"That's too bad! He's giving up the most amazing whirlpool bath."

"Let's go in." I led her into the building and opened the front door. "Please, stay as long as you'd like." I handed her the key.

Keira stepped inside. When I didn't follow, she turned. "Where will you be staying?"

"Tonight, I can stay here if you'd rather not be alone. Then I'll be at my apartment downtown."

"Well come in! How much is the rent?"

"It's a gift."

Keira hesitated. "Why are you doing this?"

"Why not?"

She turned and noticed a painting on the wall. "The Degas! What's it doing here?"

"Oh that. It arrived the same day as the "accident" at the Ramsey estate, along with a card. Just so we're clear, Eberhardt never admitted to planting the bomb. This was his way of letting me know what he'd done for you."

"What did the card say?"

"It had a symbol on it – a serpent in the shape of an S striking at a gold coin with a G imprinted on it."

"A gold coin representing the Elite and a snake representing?"

"A serpent representing the common man," I said. "Disliked and mistrusted by many. It's a creature that will strike back with full force when pressed into a corner."

Keira continued thoughtfully, "An 'S' and a 'G'."

"The letters stand for the founders of the Resistance," I explained.

She was quiet for a long time. "He didn't tell me," she said. "Not even during our last conversation. Why wouldn't he tell me something that important?"

"Secrecy is our way of life. It's the only way the Resistance can thrive."

"Maybe it's the way for the Resistance, but it's not the way between family and friends. He shouldn't have kept something that important a secret." She looked at me. "Please don't keep secrets from me, Guy. Can you promise me that?"

"I'm sorry, I can't. I won't tell you other people's secrets, and I would never tell anyone something that could compromise another person's safety. But I won't keep any unnecessary secrets from you. That's the best I can promise." Would it be enough?

Keira returned her attention to the painting. "Can you get rid of it?"

"But it's worth a fortune!" Then I noticed her expression and said, "I'll make it my second priority."

"What's your first priority?"

"You." I reached for her hand. "There are some things I promised to do for you, and I always follow through on my promises."

"What promises?"

"Well, Scott says you've never been on holiday. We can leave in a couple of weeks. Before that, I should have time to take you to a museum and to the ballet, as promised."

"Where?"

"To a museum and to the theater."

She grinned. "No, I mean where would we go on holiday?"

I smiled back. "The lake."

"The lake? As in away from the city?"

I nodded. Her smile was the only response I

needed.

-Keira-
Who Do I Want to Be?

Guy wasn't like other men I'd known. He said the apartment was a gift, but was he really giving it to me without expecting anything in return? I wanted to trust him. Guy had demonstrated trust in me by telling me about the Resistance, and I would never betray that confidence. But trusting him completely...well, that would take more time. What was important was that I wanted to give it time, wanted to give us time.

Again, he asked, "Do you want me to stay tonight?"

"Yes," I said.

In the darkening bedroom, I removed my jeans and shirt and hung them in the closet. I dug through my pack and hung up my other pants and shirts as well. After pulling a simple white tank top over my bra and panties, I decided I was ready for bed. I climbed under the comforter.

Guy waited in front of the mirror that hung over the dresser. Then he followed my example and climbed into bed wearing only his boxers.

He caressed my shoulders and back. At first, my muscles tensed. *Is this what he's been expecting? Then why didn't he...that night? No matter, it's a fair exchange for giving me a place to stay.* When I tried to roll over, he nudged me back and continued the massage. Eventually, I began to relax, and I fell asleep.

When I woke, sunlight streamed in through the open window. Guy was gone, but I found a note on the dining table.

Keira,

I had to go to work. Buy whatever you'd like for our trip to the lake. You can reach Eberhardt at 55-53-75-30. Call him for a ride when you're ready to leave. I'll stop by tonight. Dinner's on me.

Love,
Guy

Love? I picked up the pile of gats that had been left near the note and studied them. Then I took Guy's suggestion to call Eberhardt and go shopping. At noon, we stopped for lunch.

I wasn't very hungry, so I picked at my salad while Eberhardt enjoyed a triple-decker sandwich. He wasn't saying much today, so I began. One of us had to.

"Thank you."

He waved his hand. "It's nothing. I drive Guy around all the time."

"No, I mean thank you for everything else. For being my backup, for saving my life, for pulling me out of the bushes that night, and for that thing you're not admitting to." I sighed. "How can I ever repay you?"

He looked up in surprise. "You've got it all wrong. You don't owe me anything. This is my way of paying off my debt."

I shook my head. "I don't understand."

"I owe them: my wife, my children. When they needed me, I wasn't there." He set down his sandwich. "The people who did this to me." He indicated his scar. "They went after my family to get to me. Someone within the ranks...someone told them when I'd be gone. They went after my family when I was on a mission. I wasn't there to protect them. My children are gone now. They didn't survive the attack. My wife...well, everything I earn goes to pay for her care, but it isn't enough. It's never enough! That's why I helped you. That's why I do what I do. You don't owe me anything."

***

That evening, I sat on the sofa and waited for Guy. I began to sing quietly:

Yes, it's only a canvas sky
Hanging over a muslin tree
But it wouldn't be make-believe
If you believed in me.

I was willing to open up and try this wholeheartedly. Guy had helped Eberhardt when he was in a tough spot. He'd helped many others too, I was sure of it. *Who is Guy Bensen? How is it that he's always giving, without expecting anything in return? Could I ever be that selfless?* I realized then that Guy might be able to help me answer the question I'd been asking for so long. *Who do I want to be?*

-April-
A Dark Secret

Mrs. Beckett asked me to polish the windows in the sitting room today. It was another bright and sunny day, which meant I'd have to be careful or streaks would be noticed. As I worked, I watched Ashton pace back and forth across the side lawn with the push mower.

I'd heard somewhere that people used to ride mowers. It must have been nice when techno like that was available to everyone. I bet the Becketts could afford to have a riding lawn mower that worked, but they'd never allow their servants to have access to techno like that! I tried to think of a good excuse to go talk to Ashton.

I finished quickly and hurriedly put away the supplies, eager to get outside. That's when the butler approached.

"Mr. Beckett requests your presence in the study."

"Am I to bring anything?"

He shook his head, no. My sunny day clouded over. When Lance Beckett called for me, I never knew what to expect. Sometimes he wanted me for a simple cleaning job and other times...I felt a knot tighten in my stomach.

Today, it was as I'd feared. The master of the house was stressed. It was as simple as that. As he undid his zipper, I bit the inside of my cheek and willed myself not to cry. Over Mr. Beckett's shoulder, I could see Ashton mowing the back lawn. Could he be my ticket out of this madness? I closed my eyes and pretended I simply didn't exist. After what felt like forever, Mr. Beckett dismissed me.

I retired to the servants' quarters in the basement and curled up on my bed. I hated my secret. I wondered if Scott's secrets were as dark as mine. What about Keira? I knew she had secrets too. Some had even left visible scars.

I never made it outside to talk to Ashton that afternoon. I didn't feel like talking with anyone. Later, I was called to the kitchen to clean up after dinner. As usual, Lewis had prepared a plate of food for me. I thanked him but couldn't eat. I began the dishes while Lewis leaned back in his chair and pretended to read a magazine. I knew he just enjoyed watching me. At least he'd never touched me.

When I finished, I returned to my room and changed into a pair of pale pink sweatpants and a white t-shirt. Then I climbed the stairs to the first floor and crossed the kitchen to the back porch. That's where Chrissy found me. I sat on a white wicker chair and gazed at the sunset.

"Edrea and Vanessa are finally asleep. How was your day?"

"Oh, typical," I responded. "Do you like working here?"

"So far, yes. The girls keep me busy, but they're fun." She sounded sincere.

"That's good." Lance Beckett must not have gotten to her yet.

"What's wrong?"

"Nothing. I'm just tired," I said as I rubbed my shoulder. "I think I'm going to turn in early."

I returned to my room, but I didn't sleep. Why couldn't I stop him? Was this job so important that I would do anything to keep it? What if I just left? What would happen to me then? I could stay with Cole again, for a little while. Of course, that wouldn't be much of an improvement. However, the last time I'd run away and stayed with Cole, when I returned, things had gotten better for a few months.

No. I needed to be honest with myself. It hadn't really gotten better. Mr. Beckett had merely shifted his attention to the nanny. Then her "situation" had changed, and she'd left. Was I destined to suffer the same fate?

I looked around my room and remembered another bedroom, about the same size, from my childhood. After Scott had left, things hadn't changed much. Keira and I still went to school and kept house for Aunt Cady. We were together. Keira was more than a sister to me. She was also my best friend.

Then Keira had to go. Neither of us had wanted that. I wasn't ready to be an only child, and she wasn't ready to leave. She didn't even know what she wanted to do with her life, and she hadn't finished school yet. Her birthday was in November. The streets were already cold, and she was turned out with no money and no prospects. I tried to give her the money Scott had saved up for us, but she refused to take it. For about three weeks, Keira continued to go to school during the day, and at night, she sneaked through my window and slept on the floor. It was all she could think to do.

Finally, I talked to Aunt Cady and pleaded on Keira's behalf. I tried to convince her to let Keira move back in, just until the end of the school year. That's when I learned that it's a really bad idea to share secrets. My window was nailed shut and Aunt Cady made sure that when I went to bed, I stayed there. Keira no longer had a way in.

I remembered the look on her face when she stood outside my window that night. We'd held our hands up to each other. It looked like she said, "I'll come back."

She disappeared for about a month. I was worried sick, wondering what had happened to her. Then one day, she did come back. She found me at school, and we talked. She carried herself differently and had a look I'd never seen before, more wary maybe? She also had cuts and bruises and a black eye.

When it was my turn to leave, it hadn't been quite so bad. By that time, Keira had an income and an apartment of her own. We'd lived together for three and a half years. I was able to finish school, and eventually, I'd been hired at the Beckett estate.

Although I asked many times, Keira refused to tell me how she made a living. She also never told me what had happened to her when she was gone for that month. Those were her first secrets from me, I was sure of it.

When Keira told me she was going out and advised me not to wait up for her, she expected me to believe she was dating. I knew it wasn't true though. She would return in the morning silent and withdrawn. Sometimes, her clothes had bloodstains on them even when she didn't have any fresh wounds. By next laundry day, those clothes would be gone.

Over time, I figured out what Keira really did. She was angry at the world. When I finally confronted her with what I'd guessed, she no longer tried to hide it from me. My sister, the Freelancer. I'd once asked her if she was driven by hatred. She'd said no, she said she was making the world a better place. Did she really believe that?

I didn't hate anyone. I figured everyone just tried to do their best with what they'd been given. I tried my best to fit in, to find my place and a respectable job. Now, with more life experience, I wondered if there was such a thing as a respectable job for a woman, or were we all wearing masks?

At least I still believed there were some men around who knew how to treat women with dignity and respect. The challenge was to find one who wasn't already taken and who would accept a woman with little money and no status.

-Ashton-
The Resistance

The mower in front of me caught on some weeds. Today, it was not working like a well-oiled machine. I bent down to unclog the blades. When I looked up, I saw something disturbing, though it came as no surprise. I'd been informed about Mr. Beckett's hobby. It was why I was here today.

I was a Raider with the Resistance, and the Beckett estate had been chosen as our next financial endeavor. The previous nanny had approached a member of the Resistance for help. She needed a place to stay and would need neonatal health care and money to support the baby that Lance Beckett refused to admit was his. She'd been called a whore and worse before she was turned out. It was fitting that Lance Beckett would indeed be paying for the care of his youngest child.

I felt sick to my stomach. It was the maid I'd met a few days ago. She'd been friendly but had shut down immediately when I'd inquired about her boss. Apparently, she was Lance Beckett's next victim.

I decided to use this opportunity to my advantage. With Beckett's attention elsewhere, I could remove some more items from the estate. I pushed the mower toward the garage, but then turned and left it next to the porch by the back door. No one was around. The chef had gone to the farmer's market, the new nanny had left with Mrs. Beckett and the girls about an hour ago, and except for the butler who was likely taking a break, everyone else was accounted for.

I worked in the dining room today. First I took an antique bust from a marble pedestal in a cluttered corner. Then I removed a small Vermeer painting — from the way the lighting was depicted I had a good feeling that it was authentic. Last, I removed a wooden case from the buffet table. Inside was the family's best silverware. It was all I could carry.

I exited out the back door and used my hip to push the mower toward the garage. It was time to leave. I'd return tomorrow to fix the mower, finish the backyard and continue my operations on the estate. I'd need to finish within the next day or so. Other priorities now required my attention.

***

The next day I began in the garage. I'd brought some of my own tools. First, I removed the blades from the mower. Then I cleaned and sharpened them, one at a time. I'd just replaced the last one when the maid found me.

"Hello," she said with a shy smile.

I stood. "Good morning, April." I couldn't believe the outfit she was required to wear. It was degrading.

"What are you doing?"

"Sharpening the blades. They weren't working properly yesterday."

"Oh, is that why you didn't finish the back lawn?" she asked.

"Yes." I hesitated and wondered how to bring up such a difficult subject. "I noticed you."

"You did?" She looked pleased, not what I had expected.

"Yes. He shouldn't be treating you like that."

"Oh." She looked down, and her cheeks flushed. "That's what you noticed."

I gently touched her chin and brought her gaze up so it was level with mine. "Don't be ashamed," I said. "Be angry. Take control of your life. Fight back. Leave, if that's what it takes. Then fight back."

She shook her head and looked down again. "If I fight, I'll lose, and there's nowhere better for me to go. Unless..." She looked at me.

"Yes, I can help you." I nodded. "I know of a job prospect, a few actually. One is really good. It would require some training and time on your part, but it would be well worth it. It would get you out of here and in control of your own life."

"Training? What kind of a job?"

Just then the butler walked through the door. I turned to look while April instinctively took a step back and looked down.

The butler looked from me to her. "April! You were sent out here to deliver a message. Did you?"

She shook her head and stared at her shoes.

"Mr. Beckett does not like to be kept waiting. Get back to the house now and return to your duties."

April turned and ran back to the house.

The butler turned his attention to me. "Mr. Beckett would like to have a word with you in his study. I advise you to keep your hands off of his property."

Property? Had he realized that certain items had gone missing? No, I realized. The sick feeling had returned – he meant April.

I knocked on the heavy wooden door to the study. "Enter," rumbled Mr. Beckett's deep voice. I stepped into the room, and Mr. Beckett motioned to an empty chair. I sat. "I'm not accustomed to waiting for servants," he began.

"I apologize. I was in the middle of a project."

"What project?"

"The mower wasn't working properly. It needed to be cleaned and the blades sharpened."

"Is that why the lawn wasn't finished yesterday?"

"Yes, sir."

"Why didn't you clean and sharpen the blades yesterday? You didn't have permission to leave early."

"I needed certain tools to complete the job. I didn't have them with me yesterday."

He nodded. "Fair enough. I'll be docking your pay for the hours you missed. In future, be sure to check in with me prior to leaving early. Is that understood?"

"Of course, sir. I apologize for the oversight on my part."

He nodded and waved his hand. "You're dismissed."

On my way back to the garage, I took the opportunity to scope out more of the house. I was studying a painting in the hall when I sensed someone. I turned my head. April watched from a nearby doorway. She moved forward and stood beside me. We both turned our attention to the painting.

"What do you see?" I asked.

"Colors, lines, lighting..."

I smiled. She would be a good candidate for the job I had in mind, if only she'd accept. I reached down and laced my fingers through hers.

-Keira-
April, Be Careful

The day before we were to leave on holiday, I arranged to meet April for lunch at a classy restaurant near the Beckett estate. I wanted to let her know where I would be and how she could reach me. I also wanted to talk about the men in our lives.

"This is a nice place," April said. "Did you pull another job?"

I shook my head. "No, the money was a gift, and here's a gift for you." I pushed over an envelope with some money I'd set aside for her.

"Wow! Is this from Rick? Or do you call him Richard?"

"Rick." I didn't plan to tell her about the Resistance, not when her life was going so well.

"This is a lot of money. And he's giving it to me? Why?"

"Well, I'm giving it to you. It's what's left over after my purchases for our holiday. He said I should keep it."

"You're going on holiday? Where?"

"To a cabin by the lake. We'll be there for five days. You'll be able to reach me at this number." I handed her one of Richard Burke's business cards.

"Burke Investments? I knew it!" She grinned. "I knew he was rich, and he is into you, isn't he?"

"Yes, I think so."

"You think so? He must be! He's giving you presents and taking you on holiday, and he already knows what you do for a living, so it's not like he doesn't know what he's getting with you. You're so lucky to have found someone, someone perfect."

"Well, what about you? Tell me about the new groundskeeper."

"His name is Ashton." She had a dreamy look in her eyes. "He's handsome and a hard worker and...I think he cares about me."

"Well who wouldn't?" I smiled. "How long have you two been together?"

"Oh, we're just starting to know each other. What are you going to order?"

"What? Chicken, I think." I studied her a moment, then asked, "Why are you trying to change the subject? What's up?"

"Well, Ashton mentioned a new job prospect. For me," she said.

"Really? I thought you liked working for the Becketts."

"Well, I shouldn't let that prevent me from looking for something better, should I?"

"No, of course not! What is this other job? Would you be working with Ashton? I don't think gardeners get paid much more than you do, and it's seasonal work."

"No, not gardening. Ashton said it would require training. He said I'd have to be trained first, and then I would be able to support myself."

"That's all you know?"

She nodded.

"It doesn't sound like he's telling you much. April, be careful. This could be some kind of scam. Tell you what, I'll check into his background when I get back, okay? Don't make any decisions until then. If Ashton tries to hurry you into making a decision...well, that's a bad sign. Back out if he tries to pressure you."

"No, you've got it all wrong. Ashton's not pressuring me. That's not like him."

"April, you haven't known him long enough to know for sure." She avoided my gaze. It was time to back off. "I'm just trying to look out for you, okay?" I took her hand in mine. "You're my sister, and I don't want anything bad to happen to you. Now, what are you planning to order? Choose whatever you'd like. It's my treat."

-Ashton-
Taking Time Off

The next morning, most of the family and staff were absent again. I was surprised at how easy it had been to gain access to the house over the past few weeks. People were often gone or were exactly where I expected them to be, so I could easily avoid them. I had taken quite a lot. My work here was almost done. I'd even thought of an excuse for leaving, so that Mr. Beckett would have little reason to suspect me, even after I'd gone. If I could convince April to leave too, I could count this job as a complete success. I went to Beckett's study and knocked twice.

"Enter!"

"Hello, sir. There's an urgent matter I need to discuss with you." He nodded to an empty chair, and I sat. "My father has become ill. I just received word last night. He doesn't live in Tkaron, so I'll need to take a few days off to assess his situation."

"How many days?"

"Four days, give or take. I'll work late tonight and finish what I can so that the yard will be presentable until my return. If I discover that I'll need more time, I'm prepared to call you with my resignation."

Mr. Beckett pondered this for a few minutes. He rubbed his chin while he thought, then said, "I'll post the position tomorrow, and begin interviews in four days if I don't hear from you. I can't hold your position longer than that, especially at this time of year."

"I understand, sir. Thank you."

I was on my way outside when I ran into April. I'd been hoping I would see her before I had to leave. I gently took her arm and guided her into the kitchen. No one else was present. We sat at a small oak table and spoke quietly.

"Have you thought about my offer?"

"Can you tell me a little more about it?"

I had to be careful. I couldn't afford to blow my cover, but I wanted to help her very much. "Only if you accept the position. I urge you to take this opportunity."

She was quiet, and then said, "I'll need some time to think about it. Would that be all right?"

"Opportunities like this don't last. Can you let me know by the end of today?"

"No, I'm afraid that's not enough time."

I stood, reached into my pocket and withdrew one of my anonymous business cards. All it listed was a contact number. I picked up a pen from the counter, wrote my name above the number and handed her the card. "If you change your mind, call this number."

She nodded.

I walked out the back door and headed around the manor toward the front garden. As I turned the corner, I saw a familiar figure at the main entrance. I pulled back just in time. *What is she doing here?*

-April-
Laying Blame

That morning, I saw Ashton again. Funny, I thought I'd have to go out of my way to find him. Maybe he'd been looking for me? He pulled me into the kitchen. The chef was at the butcher's, so we were alone. We sat at a small table by the back window. Sunlight splashed across the table and onto the floor, making patterns. I traced some of the lines with my index finger.

"Have you thought about my offer?" he asked.

"Can you tell me a little more about it?"

"Only if you accept the position. I urge you to take this opportunity."

I had thought about Keira's advice, and Ashton wasn't telling me much. Since I really didn't know him, it would be a good idea for her to check into his background first.

"I'll need some time to think about it. Would that be all right?"

"Opportunities like this don't last. Can you let me know by the end of today?"

That certainly was high pressure. I was right to wait.

Ashton stood and reached into his pocket. He

withdrew a business card, wrote something on it and handed it to me. Then he was gone.

There was a contact number with a very light imprint in the background, a snake striking at a coin. I didn't recognize the logo. What did it mean? And who carried around business cards with no name or title on them? If Ashton knew about a legit job, he should have been able to tell me at least some of the details. I looked at the contact number again. It seemed familiar somehow.

***

The next day, Ashton didn't return to work, or the day after that. I asked around to see if anyone knew what had happened to him.

"Mr. Beckett placed an ad for a new groundskeeper and plans to begin interviews in two days if he doesn't return," the butler informed me.

"Was Ashton fired?"

"No, his father is sick. Why are you so interested?"

"No reason."

Had I made a mistake? Maybe Ashton had only been pressing me to make a decision because he knew he would have to leave for a while. Hopefully, he would return.

The butler said, "The Becketts are expecting guests for dinner. Prepare the formal dining room for six. Use the best china and silverware."

I began by spreading out a pretty white silk tablecloth. Then I looked for the silver candlesticks but was unable to find them. Instead, I grabbed a pair of crystal candlesticks. I took them into the kitchen and washed them in warm sudsy water. Then

I held them up and smiled as they sparkled in the sunlight. I returned to the dining room, inserted some pale green candles into the holders and placed them in the center of the table.

Next, I took a crystal vase and pair of garden sheers out back and prepared a pretty tulip centerpiece. As I passed through the kitchen on my way to the formal dining room, I saw that Lewis was already preparing the salad. I removed the china dishes from the display case in the far corner of the room and set out the dinner plates first, with salad plates placed neatly on top and coffee cups on saucers placed in the upper right. I carried the dessert plates to the kitchen so Lewis could prepare them for later. He joined me in the dining room and dished up the salad while I pulled open the top drawer of the buffet table and removed some pale green silk napkins that matched the candles perfectly. I folded them in a pretty design and placed one next to each plate.

I returned to the buffet table and pulled open the bottom drawer. The best silverware was missing. I pulled open the side cabinets. The silverware was nowhere to be found.

"Lewis, have you seen the silverware?"

"No, but you best get a move on." He returned to the kitchen.

I stood and looked around the room carefully. Was anything else missing? I noticed an empty pedestal in a corner. What had been there? It was a small statue, the head of a man. It was gone too. Also there was an empty nail on the wall where a small painting had once hung.

I checked the time. Lewis was right, the guests would arrive shortly, but I had enough time to inform

Mrs. Beckett. I walked up to the master bedroom and knocked lightly on the door.

"Enter!" boomed Mr. Beckett's voice.

Oh no! I pushed the door ajar and saw Mrs. Beckett finishing the knot on Mr. Beckett's tie. They both looked at me.

"Is the dining room ready, dear?" asked Mrs. Beckett.

"That's what I came to talk with you about."

"My dear," said Mr. Beckett. "Our guests will be here any minute. If there's a problem, you'd best remedy it quickly."

"Yes, sir." I fled downstairs and retrieved the second best silverware from the kitchen. Then I finished preparing the dining table and returned to the kitchen to await further instructions.

Nothing out of the ordinary happened during the meal. However, later that night, after their guests were gone, Mr. Beckett requested my presence in his study. I felt sick.

"You wanted to talk with me and my wife earlier. I think I know what about. What do you have to say for yourself?"

"What? I just wanted to report that the silverware was missing. That's why I set out the second best set."

"That's not all that has gone missing." He paused. "I see that doesn't surprise you."

I hung my head. "No, sir. I noticed a few other items were missing when I set up for dinner today."

"I expect you knew they were gone long before that, and I'll expect you to return everything by tomorrow morning."

I looked directly at him and said, "But, I don't have them! I don't know where they are!"

Lance Beckett strode toward me. He gripped me by the neck and pulled me forward so my face was mere centimeters from his.

"Then you will find them." Violently, he threw me to the ground.

I turned and tried to brace myself but cried out as the corner of my right eye glanced off the wooden arm of a chair. I hit the floor hard. Snap! *What was that?* The belt slapped across my back. I screamed in agony, but he didn't stop. He struck again and again. Tears streamed down my face and soaked the carpet beneath me.

Then Lance Beckett grabbed my upper arms and spun me around. His eyes bore into me. I had never seen him so irate, yet he seemed to be studying me. Was he deciding how to kill me?

Quietly and slowly he spoke. I felt his breath brush over my face. "She must be mistaken. There's nothing special about you," he sneered, "and now that you owe me for all that was stolen, she will never have you. I don't care how high and mighty she is. Until your debt is paid, I...own...you."

What's he talking about? Who is SHE?

But I had no more time to wonder about it. He took me then and all rational thought flew from my mind. Never before had he been so brutal. When it was over, I couldn't walk. It was painful just to stand.

Mr. Beckett grabbed me by the arm, lifted me and escorted me to my room. The door clicked shut, and the outer lock slid into place. I turned to the corner and threw up.

-Keira-
The Lake

We began our holiday at dawn. A grey hazy sky gradually brightened, turning yellow and finally, blue. We experienced little traffic along the way – some service trucks, semis transporting goods and military vehicles, very few cars.

When we arrived, rays of mid-morning sunlight fell upon the lake and made the ripples sparkle like diamonds. The falls roared in the distance. I'd never imagined anything could be so beautiful! Even the rustic cabin was perfect. We spent the day alternately talking and relaxing peacefully to a backdrop of birds twittering and wind soughing in the trees.

The first night, after we'd climbed under the covers, I leaned in for a kiss, but Guy gently pushed me back. He studied me intently for a few minutes.

"Something is different." His finger brushed against my face just over my left eyebrow where I'd been nicked by a knife. "Didn't you have a small scar there?"

"Yes, and I'm sure I still do."

"It must be the lighting. How did you get it?" he asked.

"One of my marks grabbed a brass letter opener. Fortunately, my knife was bigger."

Guy moved down and kissed my left shoulder. That scar was covered now, but he was aware of it.

"What about that one?"

"It was my first."

"Tell me about it."

"I don't really like to think about it." I pulled the blankets up under my chin and began to turn away.

"Please?"

I sighed. "It happened shortly after I turned 16. A man I was staying with burned me with his cigar. He'd laughed and told me he was branding me. He said I belonged to him. A few nights later, after he fell asleep, I made sure he understood that no one owns me."

Guy stared at me. I could sense his thoughts, but he remained silent.

I decided to answer his unspoken question. "I didn't kill him. I simply took a few of his fingers and told him they belonged to me. I figured it was a fair exchange. That's when I began making a name for myself. After that, anyone who hurt me paid for it."

Guy took my right hand and turned my arm to reveal the scar left from when I'd tried to take my own life. Even I could hardly see it. Funny, I thought it was more noticeable.

"I can guess what happened here. Do you want to talk about it?"

I shook my head, and he kissed that one too.

"May I see the others?"

I sat up, turned and lifted my t-shirt.

"There's nothing here."

"You can feel them."

He ran his fingers over my back. "Yes, there they

are." His warm soft lips kissed each scar in turn.

***

The next morning we drove closer to the falls. Their raw power was a beauty beyond words. We drove back in silence, and then ate a picnic lunch in front of the cabin. Afterward, we lounged on a blanket on top of soft pine needles and discussed the ballet we'd attended a few days ago, my first ever, when I remembered something from weeks ago.

"Guy?" I asked lazily.

"Yes?"

"Eberhardt told me that you chose your name. What does it mean? Why did you choose Guy?"

He propped himself up on his elbow and looked down at me. "I needed a new identity, for the Resistance."

I nodded.

"So I did some research. I wanted my name to reflect who I was, my new role. I read somewhere that the name Guy may come from the ancient word "guie," meaning guide or leader. That was exactly what I wanted, to guide people to safety."

"And Bensen?"

"It means warrior."

"Ah, and you're fighting the whole world."

He laughed. "Sometimes it feels that way."

-Guy-
An Evening at the Lake

That night, after a light dinner, I asked Keira if she'd like to go for a walk. This had been, by far, the most relaxing holiday I'd ever been on. Along the way, I paused to grab the blanket from the porch railing. Then we strolled along a path toward the lake. I reached for Keira's hand and gently laced my fingers through hers.

The path we followed wound through the woods and into a small glade. We continued on. Pebbles crunched underfoot as we neared the lake and found a large flat stone upon which to sit. Keira helped me spread the blanket on the ground. Then we sat and listened to the wind blow through the pine trees. We watched as black and white geese flew in a low V and settled onto the surface of the water. Keira leaned against me, and I rested my arm around her shoulders.

"They're beautiful! It's all so beautiful. I had no idea being away from the city would be like this. Thank you for bringing me here."

"Shhh..." I whispered. "Just enjoy it."

I pointed to the orange tinted sky. As the sun settled over the water, and the noise from the geese subsided, stars appeared and new noises began.

"What is that?" She sounded surprised and curious, not fearful.

"Those are frogs. It's their mating season."

"Oh, really? Are you trying to tell me something?" she teased.

"Only that those are frogs, and it's their mating season," I replied seriously.

"They don't sound like frogs."

"Not all frogs say, 'Ribbit.' Those are grey tree frogs."

"I like their call. How do you know so much anyway?"

"Education, experience and curiosity."

"Does it bother you that I have less education and very different experiences than you?"

"No, does it bother you?" I'd been learning a lot about Terene lately, precisely because of our differences.

"A little, I guess. Yes. April and I were talking about this recently. I told her I think it's wrong that some children have so little while others are given so much. She seems to think it's just the way of the world and that we have little to no control over our lives."

"April?"

"Yes, my sister, April. I'd like you to meet her when we get back."

"You've mentioned her before. Is she anything like you?"

"No, not at all! We don't even look alike. Scott and I have Dad's darker coloring, and April looks more like Mom. Her hair is long and straight and the color of honey, the color of mine right now. She's every bit the youngest. Scott and I were able to protect her from a lot, so she's usually more optimistic than me and more naïve."

A grain of concern began to sprout in my mind. "What does she do?"

"She's a maid at the Beckett estate. When I first met you, I used some of her information to try to reel you in."

I stared at the lake for a long time after that. What were the chances? I still had my arm draped over Keira's shoulders. She tilted her head back and kissed me gently on the cheek, but I didn't respond, couldn't respond, not how she was expecting me to.

"Keira, there's something I have to tell you."

She pulled away. "That doesn't sound good."

I turned to look at her in the ever deepening night. "You don't want secrets, right?"

"Right."

"I should have told you earlier, but I didn't realize the connection until just now. It's about my latest job for the Resistance."

"Guy, what is it?"

"I've met April, and she's not as naïve as you think. None of the female servants at the Beckett estate are."

Keira held still and waited for me to continue.

I sighed. "I've been working there for the past three weeks."

"You're the new groundskeeper?"

I nodded. April must have told her.

"Ashton?"

"Yes. Now that Oren is dead, I needed a new alias."

"April told me about you. Has anything happened

between you two?"

"What? No!"

"She really likes you," she explained. "Wait. What is going on at the Beckett estate? What do you mean about April not being naïve? Do you mean like what happened to the last nanny?"

"That's exactly what I mean."

"No, not April."

"I've seen what goes on there. I tried to convince her to leave, but..."

"We need to go back! We need to get her out!" Keira's eyes were wild, and her voice panicked.

"Now? Why don't we wait until morning?"

"There's no time to lose!"

I was speechless. What would the difference of a few hours make?

"Guy, don't you get it? When you steal for the Resistance, someone gets blamed. Always. I'm sure you usually let your alias take that burden so that no one else gets hurt, but who do you think Mr. Beckett is going to blame this time?"

I felt sick to my stomach. Keira was absolutely right. I'd never realized, never thought...whenever possible, I hadn't been letting the blame fall on my aliases, quite the contrary. All along I'd been hurting people too, and this time it was Keira's little sister who'd been hurt.

I stood and helped Keira to her feet.

-Keira-
Getting Her Out

During the drive back to Tkaron, Guy called someone and placed a rush order on a new identity for April. Then he tried to convince me to wait. I didn't want to wait. I wanted to get April out immediately.

"Keira, listen to me. It's possible that nobody has noticed the missing items yet, so we need to handle this delicately. If April leaves without a solid reason before that happens, Lance Beckett will suspect her for sure."

"Then we have to get her out before the robbery is discovered."

"It's not that easy. Beckett has money and power on his side. It's not just about getting April away from him. If he suspects her before we can get her out of Tkaron, he'll use the authorities against her."

"I could just take him out," I said quietly.

"How about we try to bring him down another way?"

"What do you have in mind?" I looked at him.

"I don't know yet. Just give me a minute to think." He paused. "If we can get April out discreetly, I can improve her life a great deal, and I know we can find a way to bring down Beckett in court. Remember, I have money and power on my side too."

"She said Ashton had a job opportunity for her, but...oh no! I think I convinced her not to trust you."

"You did that? She didn't jump at the opportunity like I expected. I tried to get her out the day before yesterday."

"See? These kinds of secrets, they don't help anyone. And now they've put April in danger."

"Would anyone there be suspicious if you visited her tomorrow?"

"Of course not! She's my sister. I visit her all the time."

"That's what you should do then. Stop by for a visit and convince her to trust me. I was going to call in my resignation tomorrow, but instead, I'll return to work. I'll stay on until we can get her out of the realm."

"What type of job training, out of the realm, do you have in mind for her?" I asked suspiciously.

"It's legitimate work. I know people overseas in the art world. I've been looking for someone with an artist's eye who could be trained to come back here to work for the Resistance. There are plenty of galleries downtown where April could work a day job, and on the side, she could work for the Resistance, verifying the authenticity of certain pieces before I fence them."

"April, an art dealer? Are you sure she has the right qualities?"

"She has an eye for art, and I believe she could handle the training. Do you think she'd be willing to live in Mediterra for a while?"

I settled back and tried to imagine April living a

high-class life. I liked it! As I listened to the smooth hum of the motor, I began to relax. Eventually, I dozed off. When I woke, we were back at my apartment.

***

A few hours later, I called the Beckett estate. I planned to ask April out to lunch so that we could talk privately about her options. Guy would return to the estate as Ashton the following day, the day that Mr. Beckett planned to hear from him. He would take it from there. He reminded me that it may be a week or more before we could get April out permanently. We didn't want anyone to know there was a connection between them.

Unfortunately, when I called, I wasn't allowed to speak with April. The butler informed me that she wasn't feeling well. He advised me not to stop by for a few days. He said she was contagious.

"Something is really wrong," I said after I'd closed the connection. "I don't believe for one second that April is sick or contagious. We're switching to plan B."

"We never discussed plan B," Guy said.

"Well now we're doing things my way. I'm going in today, and I'm getting her out."

"At least let me get you some backup."

"I work alone," I reminded him.

"Not on this one. I know what I'm doing. Please, trust me. Just give me a few minutes. Don't leave."

He held my gaze until I heaved a sigh and sat down to wait.

"I'll give you a ride there."

Guy took his transceiver into the bedroom and closed the door. When he returned, he wore grass stained jeans and a work shirt.

"Will I be working with Eberhardt again or with you?" I asked.

"Because we were on holiday so is Eberhardt. He isn't back yet. Let's go."

As we hurried to the car I followed up with, "Is that who you called? Eberhardt?"

"No, I called one of our Shepherds."

"A shepherd? You have some sheep I don't know about?"

"A Shepherd is what we call our operatives who are skilled at getting people from one place to another safely. It's not easy. It takes people skills and finesse and most importantly, the right contacts."

"We're really sending April away."

"Yes, if she'll go."

Guy dropped me off a few blocks away from the Beckett estate. He would wait in the car. If I didn't return within the hour, he would return to work. He was my backup. We both agreed that I, and I alone, should enter the estate on the pretense of visiting my sister who was ill. It would draw the least attention.

I approached the servants' door in back and walked right in, like usual. Lewis saw me first. He was still cleaning up from breakfast.

"Hi, Lewis!" I called my customary greeting. "Do you know where I can find April?"

He stepped in front of me. "You shouldn't be here. Come back in a few days."

"No, I heard April is sick. I want to visit her. I don't care if she's contagious."

"You need to leave," he insisted.

"I'm not going anywhere, Lewis, not until I see April."

"She's in her room, and I'll lose my job if I let you in to see her."

"Then don't let me in." I spoke quietly. "No one has to know you saw me."

He hesitated but then moved aside.

I hurried down the basement steps toward the servants' rooms. One of the doors had a lock on the outside. April never told me the Beckett's locked her in. Who would do that to the paid help? I turned the lock and opened the door.

Light from the hall spilled over a figure curled up on the bed. April wore her pink sweatsuit. I could see her maid's uniform crumpled in a pile on the floor. The room smelled terrible, like someone had been sick. Maybe they'd all been telling the truth.

"April?" I called quietly. "Are you awake?" I tiptoed closer and put my hand on her shoulder. Gently, I shook her and was surprised when she cried out in alarm. I slapped my hand over her mouth and turned her head to face me. Enormous tears streamed down her cheeks. She was really banged up. I pulled her toward me and hugged her tightly. She cringed and pulled back. What had Beckett done to her?

"Shhh," I stroked her hair and tried to calm her. "We need to get you out of here," I whispered. "Is there anything you need?"

She shook her head. I helped her stand, and we started toward the door. She could hardly walk so I pulled her arm around my shoulders to give her more support.

We were almost to the door when she said,

"Wait. Mom and Dad's wedding rings. They're on the dresser."

I returned for them, and as an afterthought, picked up her uniform.

"I don't want that!"

"It could be evidence."

"But who would you give it to, Keira? No one will believe me. I'm just a maid."

I stared at her. "April, you are not just a maid. You're so much more than that!"

I eased her arm back around my shoulders, and once again we moved toward the door.

Together, we climbed the stairs to the kitchen and had just arrived when I heard a noise from the hall. Then I felt a hand on the back of my neck. April pulled away and scooted back until the kitchen cabinets blocked her path.

"I should have known," Lance Beckett sneered. "April is too weak to have pulled it off by herself."

"What are you talking about?" I asked. "Pulled what off?"

"Where did you take my valuables? Who did you sell them to?"

"I didn't take anything of yours! Get off me! Can't you see that April is hurt? She needs to see a doctor."

"She's not going to see anyone. Who would pay the doctor's fees? She is, after all, only a maid."

While we were talking, April had risen to a standing position beside Mr. Beckett. I struggled and pulled until he turned further away from her. I wanted to give her the best chance possible to escape unnoticed through the back door, so I was surprised when she rushed at us instead and thrust her hand forward. Mr. Beckett's eyes opened wide, and he began to cough. His grip on my neck loosened. I pulled away.

He fell forward but caught himself against the countertop. I backed away. The handle of a steak knife stuck out of his back. Lance Beckett reached over his shoulder and gripped the handle of the knife. I dropped April's necklace with the rings and her uniform and lunged toward the knife rack on the counter. I turned and steadied the carving knife in my hand.

"Keira!" I heard April's scream as Mr. Beckett lunged at me.

I sidestepped but felt a searing pain in my side. I ignored it and raised my knife to his throat. Then I whispered quietly, directly into his ear, "Now the doctors won't be able to help you either, no matter how much care you can afford." April turned away as I sliced his throat.

"Grab your things!" I called as I bent to pick up the knife he'd pulled from his back. The other one was still clutched in my hand.

-Guy-
Onto Plan C

Two figures rounded the corner. One was Keira. I turned the key in the ignition, and the motor rumbled to life. Slowly, I pulled forward. When the girls climbed in, I noticed the blood drenched knives in Keira's hand. "Are we on to plan C?"

She nodded. "It was unavoidable."

I could see from April's condition that her situation had grown exponentially worse after I'd left. Lance Beckett had indeed targeted April for my actions. The skin around her right eye was red and swollen, and she walked with a limp.

I placed a call. "Can you meet us at safe house 4? Yes, as soon as possible. We're on our way." I disconnected and immediately placed a second call. "Did you get it? Good. We'll need you both on the earliest flight out. See you soon."

"Who?" I asked. I nodded at the knives.

"Lance Beckett."

"Is he?"

"Yes."

"Ashton? What are you doing here?" April asked.

"We can talk about that later," Keira murmured.

"No, Keira, now. There's nothing wrong with my

hearing or with my intelligence. Why is Ashton here?"

"There's no simple way to explain this. April, this is Rick. He was just pretending to be Ashton. You were right though. You can trust him."

"Trust him? I don't even know his name! Is it really Rick or Ashton? Or is it something else?" She was on the brink of hysteria.

Keira tried to calm her. "Listen, as soon as I learned what was happening to you, we came back."

"What was happening to me? But Ashton knew about that before you left."

"But I didn't know Rick was Ashton until last night, and he didn't know you were my sister," Keira explained.

"Last night..."

I glanced in the rear view mirror. April stared at me.

"You're Rick?" she asked.

"Yes."

"And I'm supposed to trust you? You really were trying to get me out, to get me somewhere safe before..."

"Yes," I said again. "I'm sorry I was too late."

She turned back to her sister. "Keira, why do you trust him if he lied to you too?"

"I didn't know he was Ashton, but I know who he is. I trust him and so can you. He really can help."

April looked at me again. "Why would you pretend to be a gardener? You have a good job in finance, don't you? Does this have something to do with the stolen items? Is that why Keira was hired to kill you in the first place?"

April was absolutely right. There was nothing wrong with her intelligence. My belief that our society was wrong to place value on people simply based on their monetary wealth or lack thereof was reaffirmed.

"Yes, April. I stole a lot from the Beckett estate and from Elaine Ramsey too."

She looked at Keira, then back at me. "You two are meant for each other. Do you kill people for a living too?"

"No, I work at my father's investment firm. This is a side job, and I do it to help people."

"I don't understand. How does thievery help anyone? Is there more you aren't telling me?"

"Yes," Keira and I replied simultaneously.

That was clearly not what April had expected. She turned back to Keira. "I should really trust him?"

"Yes," Keira responded. She returned her attention to me then. "By the way, where are we going? This isn't the way to the apartment."

A plane zoomed overhead as we neared the edge of the city.

"We're going to a safe house near the airport. We'll talk more there, and April, you'll have a chance to get cleaned up and changed before meeting your escort. I think I can get you out of the realm today."

"If I'm leaving Terene, I want Keira to be my escort."

"Keira cannot be your escort. She wouldn't be able to get you overseas safely. Don't worry. I've contacted someone you can trust."

"No, I wouldn't trust anyone else. I don't have the right paperwork anyway."

"Your escort will bring your new identification documents. You'll be leaving soon under a new name."

"A new name isn't enough. You'll need recent

photos."

"It's all been taken care of."

"There's a lot more you're not telling me," April said flatly. She sat back and coughed, then rode the rest of the way in silence.

I parked the car in front of a small yellow house with a white wooden swing on the porch. I turned and looked back at both of them. "We're here."

A man with a black bag stood on the front step.

"April, this is Dr. Ross. He'll need to examine you."

"Why?" asked Keira. She put her arm around April.

"We want to cover all our bases, just in case," I explained. "Please, Keira. I know what I'm doing. I've done this before."

She looked at me and then nodded.

"Are those the clothes you were wearing at the time of the incident?" Dr. Ross asked April.

She looked a little confused, so I said, "He means your uniform."

"Oh, yes."

"It's good you thought to bring it along." Dr. Ross opened a plastic bag. "It could help your case."

Keira stayed right next to her sister all the way to the bedroom door. Then April turned to her. She looked down at the knives in Keira's hands.

"I don't want you to come in during the exam." April entered the room and closed the door behind her.

Keira turned to me. Hurt emanated from her eyes. "We need to talk."

"I agree. What happened back there?"

"He attacked us from behind. He grabbed me by the neck. I tried to get his attention off of April so she could get out. She surprised me by rushing at him instead. She stabbed him in the back. I think she pierced a lung."

"You indicated that he was dead."

"Yes, I slit his throat." She held up the larger of the two knives. "He can't have survived that." Keira looked down at all the blood, and then walked over to the kitchen sink where she began to scrub first the knives and then her hands.

"What's that?"

"What?" She turned to look at me.

"That blood on your shirt. Were you hurt?" I hurried over and indicated the blood near her waist.

She looked down and lifted her shirt just a bit, to get a better look. "He must have nicked me during the scuffle. It's all right though. It's just a scratch. See?" She wiped away the blood with her shirt.

She was right, but it looked like a lot of blood for such a little scratch. Keira turned back to the sink and finished washing up.

I shook my head and sighed. "You shouldn't have killed him. We could have taken him down legally, and made a statement at the same time."

Keira looked over her shoulder. "Made a statement? By putting April through a trial? No, thank you! I'm okay with the doctor getting any evidence he needs, just in case, but that's it. We're not going to trial." She dried her hands on her jeans as she turned to face me fully.

"I decide where we go with this." I spoke quietly.

She glared at me. "I disagree."

"Do you trust me or not?"

"Yes, I trust you, but this really isn't about trust. Nobody hurts my sister and gets away with it. She's been through enough."

"Did anyone see you?"

"Lewis...the chef. And the butler knew I called earlier asking for April."

"Are they loyal?"

"I don't know. I think the butler is. I know they value their jobs."

"I'll have someone contact them, see if we can't pay them off. I can't do it myself." I continued to think aloud. "They'd recognize me as Ashton, and as far as we know, he's in the clear regarding the robbery. We'll also need to dispose of those knives."

"If you'll trust me, I can take care of that." Keira suddenly changed the subject. "You said you've done this before. You implied that you've done this before a lot. Do you always help pretty girls?"

"I help whoever I can." I spoke slowly. Surely she wanted me to help April.

"Why did you give me an apartment? What about the money? Am I just another damsel in distress to you?"

"You're no damsel in distress." I closed the distance between us and gently placed my hands on her shoulders. "I gave you an apartment because you needed a place to stay, and I know how much you liked that whirlpool bath." I noticed the start of a smile toying at the corners of her mouth. "I'm paying you a stipend because you've chosen to work for the Resistance. You should be compensated fairly for your work, everyone should. I just wish you were a little better at following directions."

"Does everyone who works for you receive regular payments, or do they get paid by the job?"

"A little of both." I shrugged. "It depends on their situation such as whether or not they have another source of income."

Keira nodded, apparently satisfied with my explanation. "Is anything going on between you and April?"

I bent down and brushed her warm lips with mine, then said, "No. When I realized what was happening, I only wanted to help her."

Keira leaned in for another kiss, and I wrapped my arms around her. When we finally pulled apart I looked deep into her eyes. "Keira, I've been wanting to ask you something."

Just then the door opened. Keira turned to look and cried, "Scott!"

-April-
Truths Revealed

After Dr. Ross took photos of the welts on my back and my battered eye, he gave me ointment and eye drops to help with the healing process and an injection to ease the pain. He was thorough yet professional.

When he left, I took a shower. Later, Keira knocked on the bedroom door. I was drying off with a fluffy blue towel.

"May I come in?" she asked.

"I guess." I shifted the towel to cover the welts on my back. She'd already seen enough.

Keira sat on the edge of the bed. "It's my turn next." She nodded in the direction of the bathroom.

It looked like she had already washed her hands, but there were blood stains at her waist and on her right sleeve. That was the hand she had used to...I didn't want to think about that.

"The doctor left. He said he thinks he has plenty of evidence to make a solid case, if we need to."

"That's good," I replied. "Does that mean I don't have to leave?"

"April, leaving has to be your choice. No one can make you go. Rick has done all that he can to provide an opportunity. It's my opinion that you should take it. Scott will go with you. He's waiting in the living room."

"Scott's here?"

"Yes, he's your military escort."

"Does he know about...about what happened to me?"

"A little. I'm sure Rick told him something, or he wouldn't be here. The doctor didn't share anything, in case you're wondering."

I sat next to her. "Keira, please be honest with me."

"About what?"

"About everything. Can't you tell me what's going on? If I decide to go, where will Scott take me? When he leaves me there, what will I do? How will I survive without either of you?"

"You'll be going to Mediterra, and you'll stay there until your training is complete. I don't have all the answers, but I'm sure Scott won't just leave you. He'll help you get settled in. Then you'll come back, and get a job right here in Tkaron."

Keira put her arm around me, and I leaned my head on her shoulder.

"You should finish getting dressed and ask Rick and Scott the rest of your questions. They promised me they'd be completely honest with you, and they're the ones who know the details. They're waiting for you."

Keira stood and opened the closet. It was full of a variety of styles and sizes of clothing for both men and women.

"Wear something light, but finish your look with layers. Go for a young rich girl look and pack a suitcase of clothes to take along too."

After Keira closed the bathroom door, I dressed in a pair of soft beige slacks and a periwinkle blouse. I grabbed a white cardigan to hide the rest of my injuries and returned to the living room. I would pack if I decided to go.

Scott and Rick fell silent when I appeared in the doorway. Then Scott hurried over and hugged me tightly. I flinched. Even with the ointment, my back felt like it was on fire. He brushed some loose strands of hair back from my face, then took my wrists and gently turned my arms so he could see the bruises.

"If Keira hadn't already, I would kill him," he said.

"Is that what you do too?" I asked.

"Only under orders, but for this, I would make an exception."

"No, don't change who you are, Scott. I don't like that a man is dead because of me, no matter how much he hurt me." I looked over at the man I knew as Ashton, "Rick, right?" He looked at Scott and nodded.

"April, I'd like to introduce you to my best friend, Guy."

"Guy? Not Richard or Rick? Does Keira know about this?"

"Yes, she does," he said. "My name is Richard Burke, as you've been told, but people I trust call me Guy Bensen. I'm one of the leaders of the Resistance."

"But that's just an urban legend! It's not real."

"I assure you, it is real," said Scott. "Guy and I formed a partnership when we were 16, and the Resistance was born. Keira just got involved recently. Now we'd like you to join too. It's a way to help people, but there are risks."

"You and Keira?" I asked Scott. I felt like I'd fallen down the rabbit hole. Ashton not being who he appeared – that I could handle – but my own brother and sister? And now they wanted me to help, but what could I do? I'd only finished high school, and all I'd been trained to do was clean and run errands. I turned my attention to Guy. "You offered me a job. It's not like what Keira does, is it?"

"Not at all. I'd like to send you to the Art Institute of Parisio to train as an art dealer. The training would take about a year, but then you could move back here and work in one of the galleries downtown or even open one of your own."

"How does this benefit you?" I asked. "How does it help the Resistance?"

"You have an eye for art," Guy said. He reached out and lightly touched the bright orange beaded necklace I'd found in a box on the dresser. "You focus on the colors, the lighting, the details. I could use someone close to home who can tell me the fair asking price for the artwork I steal."

"Why do you steal anyway? I thought you were wealthy. What do you need the money for?"

"I steal because I believe the people who cause problems should be the ones to finance solutions. The money provides salaries to key members of the Resistance and helps keep safe houses like this clean and stocked. Some of the money is used to help people get out of tough situations and back on their feet. It also covers the cost of travel, job training and false IDs."

"How does Keira fit in? How does she help the Resistance?"

"You know what she does for a living."

I nodded, my eyes wide.

"Do you think I can convince her to stop?" he asked.

I raised my eyebrows. "Good luck!"

Guy smiled ruefully. "Thank you, I think."

"No." Scott shook his head. "Smart aleck." He smiled.

"What about you?" I turned to face my brother. "Other than creating the Resistance when you were 16, I mean. How exactly do you help? What part do you play?"

"I'd like to know the answer to that too." Keira stood in the bedroom doorway. How long had she been listening?

Scott looked at Keira. "I'm a Shepherd. I use my connections and rank to provide safe transport and false documentation." Then he returned his attention to me. "Whatever it takes to keep people safe."

"Where will you be going?" Keira asked me.

"Parisio."

Scott said, "You'll learn from one of the best, Danielle Bellami. She's Guy's art dealer."

"Why would she help me? Won't I be taking away her job?"

"Not at all," said Guy. "Danielle will still be our contact in Parisio and will continue to sell our goods overseas. Having you on staff here guarantees we won't be sending her lesser quality items. She'll appreciate that." He looked at the kitchen then and asked, "Is anyone else hungry?"

***

A couple of hours later, I said goodbye to Keira, but first I turned to Guy. "You treat my sister right. It's what she deserves."

"It's what you deserve too." Guy leaned over and kissed me on the cheek.

Why couldn't I have found him first? I was happy for Keira though. I turned and hugged her tightly. I didn't want to let her go. Everything was about to change! I just couldn't say it; I couldn't say goodbye to her.

"I'll see you soon," she said as we let go of each other. I climbed into the car next to Scott and refused to look back.

-Keira-
Who Are You?

I watched as they drove away from the little yellow house. I would miss April. I knew when she returned she would be different. Her experiences overseas would change her, of that I had no doubt. I hugged myself as they drove away. Already, I felt a sense of loss even though I was both excited and a little scared for April. What would she learn? Who would she become?

Guy walked over to the porch swing, and I followed. We both sat and began to rock. He shifted and draped his arm over the back of the swing, around my shoulders, then turned his head to look at me. "Scott won't be checking in until they land, so we have the rest of the day with no plans."

I leaned my head on his shoulder. "Can we return to our holiday? You know, just leave reality behind for a while?"

"Perhaps we should bring reality more into focus instead," Guy suggested seriously.

I let out a breath. "Why do you insist on being so serious?" I tilted my head back and looked up at him.

His deep blue eyes studied me intently. "I didn't answer April's question before, when she asked how you fit in, because I wanted to talk with you about it first. How do you fit into the Resistance? How do you fit into my life? Only you can answer those questions, Keira. Who do you want to be?"

"I think about that all the time. Right now, can't I just live in the moment and think about it later?"

"No."

"No?" I pulled away from him and sat up straight. "But I can't concentrate on myself right now! I'm too worried about April."

"They're going to be out of touch for at least eight hours. This is the best time to talk about it. You're at a safe house. No one is listening but you and me. You can be completely honest here. I know who I am, and I know what I want. I came to terms with myself a long time ago. Now it's your turn. And I need to be certain of your path before we can move ahead."

I looked off into the distance. "Well, I guess I'm one of the people who breaks in and steals stuff."

"A Raider. But Keira, who are you? There's more to you than that."

I thought back. Who had I become, and why? "I was eight when my parents died. Dad from sickness and Mom from...well that's a little more complicated. As our only living relative, Aunt Cady had to take us in. I was 16, when she kicked me out. With April's help I was able to sneak back into the house to sleep for a couple of weeks. I went to school during the day but could no longer concentrate, so what was the point? After that, I lived on the streets. I had to do certain things to survive. I didn't want to, but I didn't have any other choice. I needed to eat. I needed a place to stay."

I looked at Guy. "I'd really rather not talk about

that." He remained silent, but I could tell by his expression that he wasn't going to let me off the hook. Why did he want me to talk about it, to remember? Maybe I really did need to look back before I could move forward. Guy didn't seem to be judging me, not yet anyway, but what would happen when he learned the whole truth? He already knew a little about my past, but to share all of it, to say it out loud after I'd tried so hard to forget. Would that change things between us?

I took a deep breath and continued, "A few of the men I stayed with, they hurt me, badly. I tried to drown it out with cheap alcohol. If drugs weren't so expensive, I may have tried them too. Within only a few weeks, I hit my breaking point. I almost ended it." I rubbed my wrist.

"But then I thought about April, and I knew I just couldn't, and I couldn't lose myself to the streets either. I had to fight back. It was the only way I would be able to help April when her turn came." Guy still hadn't looked away.

Now that I had started, I needed to continue, to finish this. "It was revenge at first. I hurt them as badly as they had hurt me, and I left physical signs. I wanted others to be able to see who these men were on the inside. I earned a reputation that's kept me safe, both me and April. No one on our end of town will hurt her, and even though I knew what kind of a man Lance Beckett was, I never thought he would, at least not without April telling me or fighting back. Guy, why didn't she fight back?"

He shifted his arm and pulled me closer.

"I messed up, didn't I? I didn't teach her enough. I should have taught her how to fight so that she could when I wasn't around to protect her." I began to cry.

Guy leaned down and whispered, "I know who you are. You're a fighter, a survivor. You're also a protector."

I shook my head, my thoughts still in the past. "I began hurting people as a way to survive, but then killing became a way to make a living. It's become routine. Now I don't feel anything at all when I'm on a job." I looked at him. "I would have killed you too, you know, if Elaine Ramsey hadn't slipped up. I would have killed you and not wasted another thought on it. I'm so sorry."

"Keira, who do you want to be?"

I took another deep breath. "I want to be more like you, I guess, and more like Scott, but I'm afraid for him."

"Why?"

"Scott sold out by joining the military. I really believe that. But his heart is in the right place. If the Gov ever learns what he's doing on the side, he'll be court martialed and executed. You know that, right?"

"For Scott, it was far more dangerous in the early days, when he didn't have the rank or the support that he has today, but he's brave, like you. He believed it was worth it, and he knew the risks when we started this. We both did."

"What about you?" I asked him. "I can't figure you out. You have everything: wealth, social standing. Why do you risk it?"

"Because I know who I am, and I'm being true to myself."

"And who are you, Guy Bensen?"

"I already told you. I'm a Guide. Right now, I'm your guide. So what do you think? Have we figured you out?"

"You mean, am I willing to risk it all for the Resistance?"

"I mean are you willing to work for the common good?"

I paused, then said, "Yes, but I'm doing this for more than just the Resistance."

"Why then?"

"I want to make up for past mistakes. I can't promise I won't kill again. I know I have it in me, and if I'm cornered I may have to. And I would kill to protect, but I'll try not to let it get to that point. I'll try to find alternatives."

Guy smiled.

"Who do you want me to be?"

Guy stood and pulled me to my feet. "Keira, that is the wrong question. My opinion shouldn't matter."

"But it does matter to me. I've been on my own for so long, watching out just for myself and for April, not caring about anyone else. I don't want to live like that anymore."

"And you don't have to."

Guy pulled me into a warm embrace. I leaned against him and felt his strength. When he pulled away, he reached into the pocket of his jeans and withdrew a shiny gold pendant. It looked like a serpent in the shape of an S striking at a gold coin. It sparkled in the sun.

"I know it can never replace the locket you lost, but I want you to know that I'm glad."

"About what?"

"That I was right about you."

-Scott-
No Race Can Prosper

"No race can prosper till it learns that there is as much dignity in tilling a field as in writing a poem. - Booker T. Washington."

"What?" April asked.

"That quote is what started it all."

"How do you mean?"

"I met Rick a few months before my sixteenth birthday. He was new in town. He hadn't realized who was who at school yet, so he crossed social lines that aren't typically crossed."

"You had classes together?" April asked in surprise.

"Of course not. He was placed in classes with the other rich kids, but I was sitting alone at lunch those days. I was busy trying to figure out my future. It's hard to know who to sit with at lunch, especially if you're new. Do you try to break into an established clique? Should you sit alone? Or, should you sit with someone else who looks as lonely as you?"

"I see."

"'No race can prosper till it learns that there is as much dignity in tilling a field as in writing a poem. - Booker T. Washington.' That was the first thing Rick ever said to me. He said they'd been discussing that quote in English class, and he wanted to know my opinion. At first I thought he was joking. A rich kid, asking for my opinion? I looked around to see who was watching, but no one was. No one had ever been interested in my opinion in anything before that."

"I've always been interested in your opinions," April reminded me.

"So you have." I smiled. "How are you doing?"

"I'm nervous," she admitted.

"There's an envelope in the glove compartment. It contains your paperwork: a new ID, travel documents and bank account information. Memorize the address on the ID. If anyone asks for your permanent residence, that's what you should tell them, even though it isn't where you'll really be staying. All correspondence will be routed through that address."

"Where will I be staying?"

"When you're not at the Art Institute, you'll live and work with Danielle Bellami. You should follow her instructions while you're in Parisio. She can be trusted."

"How will I know who can be trusted and who can't? I'm not used to mistrusting people. That's more Keira's style."

"Just follow Danielle's lead, and you'll catch on in no time. I think you're going to like her. You're alias is Aimee Lafleur. It will be best if you use that name from now on, especially when you return home. There's a good chance you'll be wanted, for questioning if nothing else. Beckett's family won't let his death go unnoticed."

April looked at me with tears in her eyes. "I don't

think I'll ever be able to let go of that either, Scott."

I reached for her hand. "We'll help you through this. We all will. Just don't turn yourself in. You wouldn't get fair treatment."

"Will I ever be able to use my real name again?"

"Only with people you're absolutely sure you can trust."

April nodded and opened the glove compartment. She studied her new ID, then put the documents into a purse she'd chosen from the safe house. It complemented her outfit. She really did have a flair for both style and color. If clothing styles were any indication, she and Danielle would get along well.

Other than her eye, April looked great, and even that didn't look so bad. The eye drops the doctor had given her were already beginning the healing process.

"So, what did you tell him?" April asked suddenly.

"Who?" I asked.

"Rick...Guy...what did you tell him? Your opinion of the quote," she reminded me.

"Well, I think it means that everyone is necessary. As long as a person finds some way to contribute to society, it doesn't matter which task he chooses. We're all important. That's what I told him."

"Did he agree with you?"

"Yes, and that was the beginning of the Resistance, only we didn't know it at the time."

"Scott, do you think what Keira does is necessary?"

I was quiet for several minutes. When my thoughts circled around to what Elaine Ramsey had tried to do to Keira and then to what Lance Beckett had done to April, I knew I'd found my answer.

"Sometimes. Yes."

"Oh." April looked down at her hands. "I wonder if there's another way."

"You sound like Guy."

"He'll be good for her, won't he? He'll challenge her to think about things like that?"

"Yes, he will. You know, I don't think many people are capable of doing what Keira does. It makes me feel terrible though, knowing that enough bad things have happened to her to allow her to be able to do what she does on a regular basis."

"I know what you mean."

We were both quiet for a while, lost in thought.

"April?"

"Yes?"

"I'm sorry. I thought...I mean, I didn't think he would..."

"I know. You couldn't have. I didn't tell anyone, didn't let anyone know. It's all right now, Scott. I'm safe now." April leaned her head on my shoulder.

She shouldn't be comforting me! I put my life on the line to save strangers all the time, yet I'd failed to protect both of my sisters. I shook my head. April was truly amazing. In her own gentle way, she had just forgiven me.

She was quiet for a while, and then she spoke so softly I almost missed it.

"Scott, do you think Keira focuses too much on their death?"

"Who's death?"

"Mom's and Dad's. I'm just asking because, well, look how she is and look how I am."

"Maybe, but it's more likely a result of her years on the streets and her personality. You two were always so different. That's probably why you became such good friends." I smiled at her.

She nodded. "Probably. I don't remember it at all."

"Don't remember what?"

"When they died. I think I've blocked it. I just remember snippets really, of good times with them, and then living with Aunt Cady."

April had been really little, just six. "What do you remember?"

"Mama dancing with me, swinging me around in her arms and singing me to sleep at night. Daddy telling me stories and drawing pictures – I know now that they were his architectural design plans." She smiled at me. "He would give me paper and crayons so I could work alongside him."

"He did that when I was little too."

"Sometimes they visit me in my dreams. I know they're just memories, but I like to think of them as visits."

"Those are all really good memories, April."

"It's not what Keira thinks about."

"No? Why do you say that?"

"Because she has nightmares all the time, at least she did when we lived together. She didn't think I knew, but she would call out in her sleep. And, she would say, 'They shouldn't have died like that!'"

"Yeah, she's said that to me too." I looked at April. "You think she needs to talk about it?"

She nodded. "But she never would with me."

"Maybe she'll open up more with Guy."

"I hope so."

"Or maybe he'll be reason enough for the nightmares to stop." I nodded out the window. "We're almost there."

-April-
Leaving Tkaron

The airport consisted of a large parking area, a long silver building with a lot of windows and a number of runways that spread out into the distance. Like most citizens, I'd never flown before. Air travel was reserved for military personnel with special passes, for some business leaders hoping their counterparts in Mediterra would finally share a few of their secrets and for the Elite who had family in other realms.

As I turned to open the door, Scott laid his hand on my arm. "Act like you own the place, and that I've been given the privilege of escorting you to your destination overseas. Don't defer to me, all right?"

I nodded and took a deep breath. Then I opened the door and stepped into the sunlight. Scott reached into the backseat for his duffel and the small suitcase I had packed at the safe house.

The terminal towered over us. It took all my effort to not look up, and I had to mask my surprise when the automatic doors silently slid open.

"Right this way, Miss Lafleur."

Scott gestured toward a row of check-in stations. He smiled at the woman behind the counter and reached into his back pocket for his wallet. I watched as he removed his ID and pass. I opened my purse and withdrew my own ID. I handed it to Scott and then glanced at my fingernails as if bored.

"Miss?"

I looked up at the woman. "Yes?"

"I'll need to see your travel visa."

"Oh, of course." I dug it out of my purse and handed it to her.

"Any baggage to check?"

"Nope." Scott gestured to our two bags. "We'll take them as carry-ons."

After a moment, the woman handed us our tickets. Scott returned my ID, and we moved toward the queue. At the check point, a security guard used a machine to scan our bags. He also looked at our tickets and checked our names against a list. He waved another guard over and motioned for us to follow him. A third guard took his place and continued moving passengers through the check point.

We entered a side room. A long metal table stood in the center of the room and some hard plastic red chairs lined one wall.

"Please sit." The guard gestured to the chairs.

"I will not!" I was indignant. "My father will hear about this."

Scott continued to stand next to me, but he leaned down and whispered, loudly enough for the guards to hear, "I should have warned you Miss Lafleur. They're just following procedure."

I glared at him. "Procedure? Other passengers are being allowed through the check point."

"And we'll be allowed too."

"Let me explain Miss Lafleur," one of the guards said. "Sgt. Maddock flies often, more often than most. We realize that it's part of his job, but it's also our job to make sure he's not taking anything other than you to your destination."

"But he would never! He's military."

The second guard continued, "Of course. This will just take a moment."

One guard dumped the contents of Scott's duffel onto the shiny metal table. He checked everything thoroughly.

"Step over here, Sergeant."

Scott did as he was told. He held out his arms while the guard patted him down and checked every pocket of his uniform.

The other guard opened my suitcase. The underwear I'd packed was right on top. He hesitated and looked at me.

"Just a moment." He went to the door and called to a female guard.

She entered the room and felt through my suitcase. "It's clear." She closed the lid and snapped it shut. I grabbed the handle and carried my own suitcase toward the door.

Scott gently took it from me as we rejoined the crowd. He leaned down. "I'm so sorry, Miss Lafleur."

I nodded once and looked around. Many of the people, both men and women, were in uniform. The styles differed slightly depending upon their rank. Some men wore business suits, work related travel I guessed. And there were a few families who were obviously Elite.

We sat facing the large windows. The airplanes glittered in the late afternoon sun.

"Sgt. Maddock, may I ask you something?"

"Of course."

"What are your duties, as a soldier?"

"To prepare for battle. To be ready to defend Terene at a moment's notice. And to defend our interests overseas as well. As a member of the special operations regiment, I'm also prepared to respond to terrorist threats and other unforeseeable circumstances."

"And to escort young ladies to their destinations?"

"And that."

"The security guard said you fly often. How often do you escort young ladies overseas?"

"Maybe twice a year," he admitted. "Young ladies or minors. But I also accompany my CO to the embassy in Parisio on occasion. That happens, oh, three or four times per year."

Soon our wait came to an end. We were seated in first class. Most of the businessmen and military personnel continued on back to another section of the plane. Scott encouraged me to take the window seat. The takeoff was exhilarating and the sunset beautiful.

A couple of hours into the flight, the stewardess brought us dinner. It wasn't much, but that was all right because I was too nervous to be terribly hungry. As the stars emerged, Scott explained about the time difference. He said when we arrived in Parisio, it would be morning and suggested that I try to get some sleep. I didn't think that would be possible, but I leaned my head back against the seat and tried to relax. The next time I opened my eyes, the flight attendant moved down the aisle with her cart, offering a final round of drinks.

"Two ginger ales," Scott said.

"Are we nearly there?"

"Yes, we'll be landing in about an hour. Aimee, I need to tell you something before we land."

"What is it?"

Scott hesitated, then said, "Once we land, we'll be contacting your parents to let them know you've arrived safely." He gave me a look and shook his head.

"Yes, of course." *What just happened?*

-Scott-
Parisio

I was about to tell April...I wanted to tell her, and now was probably the best time. Then I noticed the man in front of us. He tilted his head slightly as if he were interested in our conversation. My gut warned me to be careful, and I heeded the warning. I was only alive today because I had learned early on to trust my gut.

I looked at April and warned her with a shake of my head. Were we being followed? I had to assume that we were.

After a smooth landing, we exited the plane and entered the terminal. I located a public transceiver and placed a long distance call to my contact at the military base. A woman in uniform looked at me through the vidscreen.

She saluted. "How may I direct your call, Sergeant?"

"Will you please get a message to the Lafleurs? Their daughter has arrived safely in Parisio."

"It's awfully late here. Can't it wait until morning?"

"I realize it's late, but Mr. Lafleur is expecting this call."

"Yes, sir!" She saluted.

"Thank you, private." I returned the salute.

I disconnected and turned to April. She looked every bit a debutante.

"Can we go now?" she inquired impatiently.

"Yes, of course, Miss."

I picked up our luggage. After about 20 paces, I cleared my throat, and she turned around with an impatient look.

"Is anyone using the transceiver we just left?"

She turned back around and kept moving. "Yes, the man who was sitting in front of us on the plane."

It was as I'd expected. He was probably tracing the last number dialed. He would discover that I had used a legitimate military number.

I led April toward the baggage terminal. We sat and pretended to wait for more luggage. When I was certain we were no longer being followed, I looked at April.

"There's a claim number in your purse with your other paperwork. May I have it?"

April dug through her purse and handed it to me. I approached the message station. "Was anything delivered for Art Fantastique?" I asked and handed the young man the claim ticket.

He scanned the small teleview in front of him. "Yes, your packages are right over here, sir." He led us to a cart.

I set our luggage next to the packages and pushed the cart toward the line of taxis that waited outside. April followed. A porter helped me load everything into the trunk of a cab. I tipped him, and he returned the empty cart for us. I helped April into the backseat of the cab and slid in next to her.

She gazed out the window as we drove away

from the airport. "The cars look different – smaller, cleaner, well maintained. And Scott," she whispered, "where are the wheels?"

"They're hovercars," I whispered back. "They float."

"Wow!"

"Art Fantastique, s'il vous plait," I instructed the driver.

April stared out the window. She took in everything – the cleanliness of the streets, the hovercars and the maglev trains on either side of the highway.

She turned and gave me a careful look. I couldn't quite read her expression.

"What is it?" I asked.

"We lost the war, didn't we?"

"Yes."

She nodded sadly. "They didn't teach us that in school."

"Of course not."

"You've been here a lot, to Mediterra, I mean. Haven't you?"

"Yes."

"And you transport people and goods."

"That's right."

"Do you bring the people here because it's better?"

"No, that's not the agreement, but we can talk more about that later."

"Have you wanted to stay?"

"Yes. No. I have reasons to stay and reasons to go, but for now, I can do more good back home."

April nodded slowly and returned her attention to the streets and buildings of Parisio.

-April-
Welcome Home

The cab made its way down a back alley and stopped behind what I presumed to be Art Fantastique. Scott told me to wait while he unloaded the packages. Then he climbed back into the cab, and gave the driver further instructions in another language. Eventually the cab pulled to a stop in front of a building with a beautiful stone facade. I had never before seen buildings quite like those in Parisio. They looked old and majestic yet were in excellent repair. Scott offered his hand and helped me out of the cab.

"Welcome to your new home."

"I'll be living here?"

"Yes, what do you think?"

"I don't know. Alone?"

"No, not alone." He smiled, reached for our bags and ushered me up the front steps. At the top, he turned to a keypad and punched in a series of numbers. I heard a metallic sound as the lock released. Scott pushed open the heavy wooden door.

I stepped inside and looked around. Even though the outside of the building looked different than what I was used to, the inside looked very much like wealthy homes in Tkaron. An ornate wooden chair stood next to a coat rack and umbrella stand in one corner of the front hall. A winding staircase led up to the second level. Arched doorways led to other rooms. Through the one on the left, I could see a small dining room, and a parlor was to the right.

The click of high heels sounded on the polished wooden floor as a woman approached us from a hall behind the staircase. "Ah, vous avez arrivé!" She smiled and walked directly to Scott.

He opened his arms and embraced her warmly. Then he kissed her gently and used words I couldn't understand, although I knew he was talking about me. "C'est ma soeur, April, mais son alias est Aimee." He kept his arm around her as they turned toward me. "April, I'd like you to meet Danielle Bellami, my wife."

Did he say wife?

"It's a pleasure to finally meet you," Danielle responded with a thick accent. She took my hand and kissed me first on one cheek and then on the other. "I'm so very happy to finally meet Scott's family."

I looked at Scott. "Is this what you were going to tell me on the plane?"

"Yes, but it wasn't safe to talk."

"That's right! Why was that man following us? I thought nobody knew I was here."

Danielle looked at Scott and said, "You were followed?"

"Only in the airport, not after," he replied, and then turned to me. "I don't think they were following you, April. Let's move to the sitting room." Scott gestured to parlor. "It's been a long trip."

As we moved into the stylish yet comfortable

room, my head spun. *Scott is married?* I'd been sitting for too long, on the plane and in the cab, so I stood instead.

I looked at Danielle. "I apologize for my reaction. I don't mean to be rude. It's just...this is the first I've heard about Scott being married." I looked at Scott next. "Is this what Keira was talking about that day in the park?"

"I don't know what you mean." He looked baffled.

"She was mad at you for keeping secrets. Don't you remember?"

"No." He shook his head. "That was about the Resistance. Keira doesn't know about Danielle. No one back home does."

He and Danielle sat side-by-side on the sofa. Her hair was just about the same color as his. It was tied up in a loose bun and tendrils ran along the sides of her face, enhancing her olive complexion and deep brown eyes.

Danielle looked at me. "I'm sorry. I expected Scott to tell you before you arrived. Do you want me to leave so you two can talk privately?"

Scott put his hand on her knee. "No, you should stay."

"How long have you been married?" I asked.

"A little over a year. Our anniversary was just a few weeks ago. April, please sit."

I perched on the edge of a cream colored chair, and he continued, "I met Danielle when I began transporting people and goods overseas for the Resistance. That would have been about three years ago."

"But, you've been a...a Shepherd, right?"

He nodded.

"For much longer than that, haven't you? Since the beginning?"

"No, the Resistance grew slowly. It took time to develop trust with others who felt as we did and for all of us to get into positions where we could support each other properly. The person I called from the airport, for example. Her role is to relay messages. She'll let Guy know we arrived safely. The man who was following us?"

I nodded.

"He called her after I disconnected, I'm sure of that. No matter how high his level of clearance, our Messenger would verify that I was sent to escort Mr. Lafleur's daughter to their family overseas."

"But what if he checks into that? There's no record of an Aimee Lafleur, is there?"

"Yes, there is actually. We have people with all types of skills helping the Resistance. Aimee Lafleur exists in the national data banks, along with enough background details to convince anyone. If our tail calls the numbers that are listed for Aimee Lafleur or her parents, he'll be connected to someone who knows exactly what to say to keep you safe."

"Wow..." I sat back. "How could you have possibly kept all of this a secret from Keira and me?"

"That was the most difficult part." Scott leaned forward and took my hands. "I wanted to tell both of you, especially about Dani. But I couldn't, not without telling you about all of it, and how could I do that without disrupting your entire life?"

"You need to tell Keira about Danielle," I said softly. "There's no reason not to now."

He nodded and sat back. "You're right. It's time for the secrets between us to end."

-Scott-
No More Secrets

When I returned to Tkaron, Keira invited me over to her new apartment for dinner. I was a little surprised, Keira wasn't the best cook, but privacy was likely the reason. We would be able to talk freely during dinner.

I knocked.

Even as Keira opened the door, she asked, "How's April?"

"She's fine," I said and closed the door behind me. "Is Guy here yet?"

"No, he should be here soon though."

"Good. I was hoping I'd have a chance to talk with you alone. Can we sit?"

"Sure." She gestured to the sofa. "What is it? What's wrong?"

"Nothing's wrong. I'm just not sure how to tell you this." I looked down and took a deep breath.

"Scott?"

I lifted my head and looked at her. "Keira, you know I've been keeping secrets."

"Yes, about the Resistance, and I know you must have some military secrets too."

"There's another secret, a big one...one I've been

keeping from everyone. I've told April now, and I want you to know too. I've wanted you to know since the beginning, but..."

She waited patiently.

I'd just have to say it. "I'm married. I've been married for just over a year."

"What? To who? Why would you keep something like that a secret? Aren't weddings supposed to be happy occasions? You know, something you would invite your sisters to?"

"Yes, they are, and we are, very happy, when we get to be together."

"When you get to...is she military, stationed somewhere else?"

"No, but she lives really far away."

"I see." She nodded. "She's Mediterran, isn't she?"

"That's right."

Suddenly Keira punched me in the arm, hard.

"Ow! What was that for?"

"For keeping secrets! How can I be happy for you if you won't tell me about the best parts of your life? Who is she?"

"Some secrets are worth keeping, Keira. You must realize that, and you mustn't ever tell anyone about this. It would kill me if anything happened to her."

Keira sat back. "You can trust me, Scott."

I nodded. "I know. Her name is Danielle Bellami. She's Guy's contact overseas and April's mentor."

"Do you have a picture?"

"Yes, April said you'd want to see what she looks like." I pulled out my transceiver and brought up a small image. I studied it briefly, then handed it to Keira. It appeared that Dani was looking right into my eyes. She was smiling, and her long dark hair was blowing off to the side.

"She's pretty. Will I ever get to meet her?"

"I don't know how."

I shook my head as I took the transceiver from Keira and deleted the image. The wrong people must never discover my ties to Dani.

"I've been trying to think of a way, but it's pretty risky traveling overseas right now. She was going to come here for our anniversary, but with everything that's been going on lately...I've been tailed more often than not...it's just not safe. Security is getting tighter and tighter. I don't think I'll be able to get you through for a while, not to see April and not to meet Dani."

Keira took my hand. "Well, I'm happy for you because you've found someone to share your life with, and I'm sad for you because she's so far away. Wait here a minute, I have something for you."

Keira went to her bedroom and returned with Dad's book of poetry.

"Thank you for letting me borrow this. Maybe you could read some of the poems to Dani."

Just then, we heard a key in the lock. "Let me be the one to tell Guy," I insisted.

Guy saw us and smiled. Then he frowned. "What's burning?"

"Oh hell, the vegetables!" Keira jumped up from the couch and ran into the kitchen. "Well, these are no good anymore," she called. "Salad, anyone?"

We sat down to eat, and I looked across the table at Keira. "Thank you for dinner."

"You may regret those words." She shook her fork at me.

"How was your trip?" Guy asked.

"We were searched, thoroughly. They said it was routine, but it felt different. They've begun tracking my flights."

"Did the artwork get through?"

"Yes, it's all been delivered, but I recommend you send someone else to deliver the next batch."

"What about April?" Keira asked.

"Like I said, she's fine. She's settling in nicely at Danielle's. Her classes at the Art Institute will begin in a few weeks – summer session. Until then, she'll shadow Dani and begin learning the language."

"Why don't you tell us a little more about Dani." Keira suggested. She took another bite of her salad.

She was right. I shouldn't put it off any longer. "Guy, I want to thank you."

"What?" Guy was having trouble cutting through his steak. He gave up and looked at me. "Why?"

"If it hadn't been for you, for your plans to make allies overseas, I never would have met Danielle, and we never would have gotten married."

"Married? Do you really think that's wise?"

"Wise or not, we were married over a year ago, and we've been able to make it work."

Guy pushed back his plate. "But now they're tracking your flights."

"Yes."

"We'll have to try to do something about that, won't we?" Guy said.

"I'd like us to work on it, yes."

"Let's forget the steak," Keira suggested, "and celebrate with some apple pie."

-Keira-
Keeping Busy

I was glad April was settling in nicely in Parisio. Weeks passed, and in many ways, I was settling in nicely too. I loved my new apartment, and I saw Guy almost every day. Some days we had lunch together. Sometimes he would spend the night. Most of the time, I was free to do as I pleased, just as I always had.

I continued one of my favorite past times, people watching. I enjoyed being in different settings, watching how different people reacted to the events in their lives. I drew on this knowledge whenever I pulled a job.

But I hadn't pulled a job since we'd rescued April, and I was getting restless. To be fair, I didn't think Guy was currently working undercover either. He seemed happy enough going to work at his father's firm and spending much of his time off with me. But eventually, I started asking.

"Have you thought of a way to help Scott?"

"What do you mean?"

"He needs a way to be able to fly to Parisio, regularly."

"He knew the risks well before he married

Danielle."

"Don't you want them to be together?"

"I help people who are truly in need of help. Scott and Danielle are both healthy and safe."

"But you told him you'd try to help!"

"Let me and Scott worry about that, all right?"

"Well, do you have anything else going on? Is there anything I can do to help the Resistance?"

Guy sighed. "No, nothing right now. Keira, you'll have to be patient. Weeks can go by between jobs, sometimes even months, and it is better that way, safer. I'll let you know when the right job comes along."

I sighed too. "All right."

"Look, why don't you learn a new skill? Why don't you ask Eberhardt to teach you how to drive?"

"You want me to learn to drive?"

"Knowing how to drive is a good skill to have. Don't you agree?"

"Sure. All right. I'll talk to Eberhardt tomorrow."

Driving was fun – more fun than I had expected, but it wasn't what I craved. A couple more weeks went by with nothing, no jobs for the Resistance. Apparently, all was right with the world. That should have made me happy, but...

"Couldn't we go looking for a job? I'm sure someone needs help," I said to Guy one evening. "Besides, I need to keep my skills sharp, and I need to have some fun."

"Aren't we having fun?" Guy tickled my neck with the tip of his tongue.

I playfully pushed him away. "Yes, but I mean a different kind of fun."

Well, we had fun that night, but not the kind I'd been talking about. Finally, I remembered what I'd told myself so many weeks ago. I could work for the Resistance and still pick up bounties on the side.

***

The next night Guy and I didn't have any plans together, so I decided not to stay home. I wore a classy skirt that revealed plenty of leg, a red top with a drop neckline and a pair of black heels. I took a minute to admire my reflection in the mirror, then headed out.

The Dry Martini was the sort of place where business men went to relax after work. In my experience, disgruntled workers were easy targets, and this was the perfect place to find them.

I chose a seat at the bar where I could see most of the patrons in the mirror. I ordered a martini and listened to the conversations that flowed around me. Almost immediately, I noticed a man in a dark grey suit. He was complaining to an associate about one of their competitors.

I looked for an opening. Another man in a tuxedo sat at a piano in the middle of the room, and though a number of people were dancing, the parquet dance floor was not overly crowded.

I stepped down off the bar stool and made my approach.

"I love this song," I gushed and looked directly at the man in the grey suit. "Don't you?"

His friend nudged him with his elbow.

"Uh, yes." He cleared his throat. "Would you like to dance?"

"I'd love to!" I took his hand and let him lead me to the dance floor.

As we swayed to the music, I moved closer. He

smiled. I gently nuzzled his earlobe and whispered, "What do you need?"

"What are you offering?"

"To help you move up the chain of command."

Startled, he began to pull away. I leaned my head on his shoulder. "Don't. You'll draw attention."

He moved close again, and we continued to dance.

"I overheard you and your friend talking, and I believe I can help. What would allow your company to move ahead of your competitor and also impress your boss?"

"Who are you?"

"It's better that you don't know, especially if you decide to hire me, but you didn't answer my question. Why don't you take some time to think it over? I'll be here again tomorrow, same time." The song ended. I kissed him lightly on the cheek and thanked him for the dance. Then I turned and walked away.

***

The next evening, I returned to The Dry Martini. My mark stood at the bar looking just a little nervous. He hadn't spotted me yet. As I walked past, I discreetly took his wallet.

I chose a seat at a small round table, checked his ID and waited for him to notice me. A few minutes later, he sat down.

I smiled. "You've decided to accept my offer." It wasn't a question.

"I'm not sure."

I rested my hand lightly on top of his. "Yes, you are."

"How much would something like this cost?"

"It depends on your needs."

He reached into his pocket, then handed me a rumpled business card.

"Cybonautics – the security company?" I looked at him, and he nodded.

"That's the president of Cybonautics. I'd like his data processor access codes. Can you get them for me?"

"40,000 gats," I suggested.

"That seems steep. How about 20?"

"Have you ever done anything like this before?"

He just stared back.

"35? The payoff for you would be well worth it." I paused to let that sink in.

He narrowed his eyes. "30 thousand."

"Done. No payment will be due until the job is complete."

"If I don't need to pay until the end, why would I pay you at all?"

"You didn't really just ask that. Did you?"

"You're willing to take the job, and you don't even know who I am."

I smiled and held out his wallet. "Brody Delaney, soon to be executive officer of CalTech Security, if you don't blow it."

He reached for his wallet and began to thumb through it.

"Everything is there, minus one business card." I held it up. "I'd like to keep it, if you don't mind."

He nodded once. "I accept your terms."

"Then we have a deal. In two weeks, we'll meet back here, at say...7:00? I'll bring you the codes, and you'll bring me the money."

"Why so long?"

"Long? For a job like this? The president of a security company...stealing the codes from his office would be close to impossible as a solo mission. I'll need to get into his house. Even that will be tricky. I need time."

"You're sure you can do this?"

"I can, and I will." I smiled. "How about another dance?" It felt good to be back in the game.

He stood and held out his hand. I placed my fingers gently onto his palm, and we moved onto the dance floor.

-Keira-
A Job Gone Wrong

It was nearly midnight when I walked upstairs from the servants' quarters. Gaining access to the house had been fun. The butler liked to play drinking games at a local pub on his night off. I'd won, of course. He was having so much fun that I doubted he even realized he'd brought me home. At least he remembered the passcode to get back into the manor. I smiled. Guy would be pleased that I hadn't been hired to kill.

Silently, I moved through the kitchen and down a dark hallway. The moon offered the only light. Even so, I had no difficulty finding the office on the first floor. *But what's this?* An unexpected silhouette cast a shadow against the far wall. The safe was open and the person appeared to be writing something in a notebook.

Without a sound, I crept inside the room and lowered myself against the wall. I needed a minute to think. Who else wanted those codes? There weren't too many companies in the line of security. Had someone else also hired a Freelancer? *What were the chances? What are my options?* I could just wait and then retrieve the codes for my client too.

When the shadow closed and locked the safe, I got a good look at it. *Damn, it's one of the high techno kinds. I don't think I'll be able to crack it.*

The shadow turned toward the door. From this angle, I could see that she was a young woman. Chances were good that she had the codes I needed. I would have to follow her and...

She reached the door and was just about to step into the hall when she hesitated. Then she turned and looked directly at me. I stood. We studied each other for a moment.

"You're good," she said. "I didn't hear you come in."

"So, what are we going to do about this?" I asked. "Are you willing to share?"

"Well, we don't want to draw any attention."

"I agree."

"But I can't let you take anything."

"Why not?" I looked at the papers in her hand. "You did."

"If we leave quietly now, no one will know that anything was stolen. That's the way it needs to be."

"I believe we've come for the same thing. What would be the harm in both of our clients gaining access to the codes?"

She shook her head. "I don't think my client would like that."

"He wouldn't need to know, and we'd both get paid."

She began to move, to circle around me. I moved with her, keeping her in front.

"Who hired you?" she asked.

"Who hired you?" I responded in kind.

Suddenly, she stopped. I realized a fraction of a second too late that I'd been played.

A meaty hand clamped onto my wrist, spun my arm behind me and put me in a neck hold. Just. Like. That. It was embarrassing.

I was dragged down the hall and outside. I wondered why the alarm didn't go off, and then realized they must have disabled it. Two blocks later, we stopped, and I was shoved into the backseat of a car, a car I recognized instantly.

I snorted. "I'll drive." I turned my head toward the man and the woman. "No names," I suggested.

Eberhardt nodded and surprisingly, let me drive. The woman deferred to his judgment.

"Where to?" I asked.

"You can drop me off at A Shot in the Dark," she said. "Do you know where it is?"

I nodded and started the car. I put it into gear and gently pulled away from the curb. My mind was reeling, but my business in this matter was with Guy, not with the girl.

After we dropped her off, Eberhardt turned on me. "What the hell were you doing back there?"

"The same thing you were, apparently."

"But why? You work for the Resistance now."

I turned my head away from the road and stared at him just long enough to make my point. "Work for the Resistance? What work have I been given to do exactly? It's not like I haven't asked! I need to keep my skills sharp. I need to keep in practice. What would you have me do?"

"Train with me," he suggested.

"What?"

"I know what you're going through. Do you think I just sit around in the car all day?"

I shook my head, surprised at his outburst.

"I get it. You're bored. You want to be where the

action is. So come train with us."

"Us?"

"Yes, the other Raiders and me. We practice regularly, to keep our skills sharp."

I pulled into the garage beneath Guy's apartment and stopped the car. Then I turned to face Eberhardt completely.

"What about keeping everyone's identity a secret?"

"Yes, that's important too, but it's also important to practice working together. Remember what I said about backup?"

I nodded.

"We practice in small groups," he continued. "None of the Raiders know all of the other Raiders, and most of them have never met Guy, but we do form networks. To start, you can work with me and the girl you met tonight."

"Thanks, I guess. I might just take you up on that. But..."

"What?"

"Why didn't you tell me about this before?"

"I should have. It's just...Guy didn't want it that way. I've got your back now though." He exited the car, and then walked around to open the door for me.

What a strange thing for him to say. I thought he already had my back.

We entered the apartment, and Eberhardt dropped into the first chair he came to. Guy was on the couch. He put down his book when he saw me.

"Keira! I didn't expect to see you tonight." He started to stand, but I pushed him back down. Then I sat on his knee and put my arms around his shoulders.

"Guy, what were you thinking?" I asked sweetly.

"What do you mean?"

"Why didn't you send me in tonight?"

He sighed. "Keira, it wasn't the right job for you. I didn't want you to get hurt. I care about you."

"Wrong answer!"

"What? It's wrong for me to care about you?"

"Don't try to change the subject. If you cared about me, you would have sent me in tonight. I've been asking for a chance like this for weeks now!"

"Well, it's not like I sent another woman in."

"Whoa! Wrong again!"

Guy hesitated and looked at Eberhardt. "Is there something you neglected to tell me about Ricardo?"

Eberhardt finally spoke up. "Guy, everyone knows you don't like to send in the girls."

"I didn't know that," I muttered.

"And some of these girls are really good at what they do."

"But I second that! Guy, you really need to give me some challenging work, or I'll find work elsewhere. Speaking of which," I looked at Eberhardt, "I'll need a copy of those codes."

Guy pushed me off his lap, and I landed on the cushion next to him. "Keira, what did you do?"

"I took a job from someone who trusted me to do it right." My tone was like ice. "He's getting the codes."

"Do you have any idea what those codes are for?"

"Security protocol."

"And how does your client plan to use that information?"

"He works for CalTech. He wants to move up. That's all. How do you plan to use the information?"

"It will give us Intel into the security systems that Cybonautics uses."

I shrugged. That didn't mean much to me, although I recognized the name from the business card Brody had given me.

"It's the firm in charge of security at the major airports. Having access to these codes means the Resistance can assure safer passage for our members, including Scott, including April, and..."

"And what?"

"I thought I was right about you." Guy shook his head, stood and walked to the window. I sat in stunned silence.

-Guy-
Trust

Eberhardt moved to join me at the window. He placed his hand on my shoulder and spoke quietly so Keira wouldn't hear. "Does my opinion mean anything to you?"

I nodded.

"You were right about Keira, but your feelings for her are clouding your judgment. If you're not careful, you'll lose her. I suggest you try getting even closer. Trust her with more." He left then.

I continued to stare at the night sky. The latch clicked as Eberhardt let himself out. It wasn't a new thought. I'd considered trusting Keira with more, but after this... Was it really my doing, or more accurately my inaction, that had driven her to take another job? I took a deep breath as I thought about that and made my decision.

I turned, but Keira was no longer on the sofa. I sensed movement as the front door closed without a sound. My heart jumped to my throat. *Not again!* I wrenched open the door. She was already partway down the hall and gaining speed.

"Wait!" I called, and Keira froze. "Don't go. Please don't."

She turned and looked at me. Her black clothing almost allowed her to disappear into the darkness of the hallway. Almost, but not quite. Her eyes glistened.

"Don't run away again. Please don't go down that road. Can't we talk?"

Cautiously, she approached me, and I heaved a sigh of relief.

"Keira, I was right about you. I'm sorry I said otherwise. Please come back inside. There's something I've been wanting to tell you."

She followed me in and walked to the window. I stood beside her but not too close.

"What I really meant to say before was that the job tonight...there's another reason I didn't want you in on that. It's a gift for you – a way for you to be able to visit April in Parisio."

She turned her gaze to the stars. I couldn't quite read her, so I simply waited.

She didn't look at me when she spoke. "May I have the codes for my client? I don't like to break contracts, even verbal ones. It's not good for my reputation, and I don't think it would mess up your plans."

"It could."

"How so?" She turned to look at me.

"Cybonautics may discover that another company has learned their trade secrets. It could ruin them."

"So CalTech would be in the lead. Would that really change anything for us? Couldn't it even help? Best case scenario, we form a partnership with CalTech. I could, anyway, especially if I help my client get to the top. Or, think about this. Let's say Cybonautics retains their contracts with the airlines. If people are caught sneaking through security or messing with the codes, we could make sure that blame is placed on CalTech and divert attention away from the Resistance."

"I don't know. Your ideas involve a lot of unknowns."

"Life involves a lot of unknowns."

"Let me think about it."

She nodded. "All right. May I stay here tonight?"

"Why? So you can sneak out of bed in the middle of the night to record the codes?" *What was I doing?*

"No!" She looked hurt. "Is that why we always stay over at my apartment? Because you think I'll poke around through your things?"

"You did when we first met."

"I didn't know you then – you were just a mark." She stepped away from me. "I thought you trusted me."

I took Eberhardt's advice and stepped toward her, closing the gap between us. "I do, but I need you to make me a promise."

She looked at me warily.

"Can you promise you won't run from me again? Promise me, if you decide to leave, you'll tell me you're going and tell me why."

She hesitated, and then sighed. "Okay, I promise."

I held out my hand. "Will you come with me?"

I had made my decision. I walked her over to the desk and opened a secret compartment in the top left hand drawer. I retrieved a key on a short chain and lifted it so that it dangled in the space between us.

"You're welcome to stop by anytime, at any hour. Will you be my partner in the Resistance?"

She reached out her right hand, palm up, and I

placed the key in it. Her fingers curled shut.

I didn't lock up the security codes that night. Instead, I put them in the secret compartment. Then I turned to Keira. "Shall we retire for the night? It's been a long day."

She nodded and went into the bedroom. I followed her and watched as she removed her jacket, shoes and pants. Black lace underwear – I'd expected as much. She left on her t-shirt and climbed under the covers.

I removed my clothes down to my boxers, and climbed into bed beside her. I laid down on my side with my head propped on my hand. I wanted to take her in my arms, but I was hesitant to press her after she'd so nearly fled. That brought some other questions to mind – questions I wasn't sure I wanted answered, yet still felt a driving need to ask.

"Keira, when you run, where do you go?"

"Somewhere familiar, somewhere safe."

"But who do you stay with?"

She turned to look at me. "Do you really want to know the answer to that?"

"Not specifics, I guess, but I want to understand you."

She hesitated, and then let out a breath. "There's a man, a man I know won't hurt me. He allows women to stay with him, for a fee."

She studied my face. I tried to mask jealousy with a calm passive look.

"Do you trust him?"

"I trust him to keep me hidden when that's what I need."

"Does he love you?"

"No."

"Do you love him?"

"No," she said, without hesitation.

I nodded. I'd heard enough. I turned off the bedside lamp. There was a sick feeling in my stomach, but I had asked, and she had responded with the truth. I wouldn't want it any other way. Keira rolled over, and I reached out to hold her. She shifted back into my arms.

I couldn't sleep. I thought about my recent decisions and how they would impact my life. Without realizing it, I began to gently stroke Keira's arm, so I was a bit surprised when she turned toward me and responded completely and without inhibition. As she settled onto me, I heard a sigh in the darkness as well as something I'd never heard from her before.

"I love you, Guy."

-Keira-
The Dry Martini

Guy decided not to go to work the next day. Instead, we discussed something important over breakfast – whether or not I should give the Cybonautics data processor access codes to Brody Delaney.

"He's in a position to become a strong ally, if we play him right."

Guy studied me. "But can you play him right? How can you be sure that you can control him?"

"Nothing is ever sure when it comes to other people," I reminded him, "but I think I can do this. And even if I can't, we could use CalTech as a scapegoat if necessary."

"How much time do we have? When are you supposed to give him these codes?"

"Tonight, 7:00."

"How much did you charge him?"

"30,000."

Guy whistled. "Not bad!"

I smiled. "You know I'm good."

"Yes, I do." He smiled too. "I have an idea. Let's extend an olive branch."

"What do you mean?"

"Give Delaney a discount. Reduce your fee to 25,000, stroke his ego and only his ego..."

I laughed as Guy continued, "And begin building a friendship. Just don't push it too far. If he falls for you, or thinks you're offering more than you are, and you have to dash his hopes later, this could backfire on us."

"Will do, boss!" I saluted him.

"Don't do that." He rolled his eyes.

This was perfect! Finally, Guy trusted me to do what I did best.

***

That afternoon, Eberhardt drove me to an empty field on the outskirts of Tkaron. Ricardo was already there, her long dark hair tied back in a ponytail. A bicycle was on its side a few meters away. I exited the car and stood facing her in the warm sunshine.

"Keira, this is Raquelle, but the other Raiders know her as Ricardo. Raquelle, this is Keira, sometimes known as Madeline."

"Oh, not anymore," I corrected. "That ID blew up, remember?"

"Blew up, huh?" Raquelle and I shook hands, and I smiled at her.

"Ladies, shall we begin with a few warm up laps?"

We both nodded and began to run.

After a half hour high intensity workout, the real training began. Eberhardt taught me how to safely use and dismantle a handgun, while Raquelle practiced target shooting nearby. I tried to tell Eberhardt that guns leave too much evidence behind, but he pointed out that even if I chose not to carry, someone could pull one on me.

Next he emptied the gun, and we took turns disarming each other. This, I felt, was a far more useful skill. When I'd needed to in the past, I'd fought with sheer gut instinct. It felt good to learn some of Eberhardt's trusted techniques.

We agreed to meet again in two days at Eberhardt's apartment where Raquelle would begin to teach me the fine art of disarming high techno security devices, an extremely useful skill for a Raider.

On the way home, Eberhardt let me drive again. "Thank you for inviting me along today."

He just nodded.

"It was you, wasn't it? You saw me enter the room after Raquelle last night. You let her know I was there."

"Yes, but I didn't know it was you."

"You're good backup, Eberhardt."

He smiled.

***

When I opened the door to my apartment, a wonderful aroma welcomed me.

"What's this?"

Guy turned from the stove. "An apology dinner. I really am sorry about some of the things I said last night."

I kissed him on the cheek. "You're forgiven. Just let me go clean up."

"Clean up after," he suggested. "Sit and eat now. The food is ready."

Guy pulled out a chair for me, and I sat.

"Did you really cook this, or did you have it

catered in?" I teased. "It really is better than anything I could make."

He shook his head. "It's really not much. You just haven't taken time to practice."

"Maybe you could teach me?"

After dinner, I showered and prepared for my meeting with Delaney. Guy walked into the bedroom just as I was clipping up my golden curls.

"You're wearing that?" He stared at my short black cocktail dress. The deep V-neckline and sequined clip at the waist drew the eye right past my breasts.

"Is something wrong with it?"

"Try this." He held up a glittering necklace that matched the clip at the waist. "It will draw his eyes back up to your face which is exactly where we want his focus to be."

I held up my hair, and he fastened the clasp. Guy was right. It was the perfect finishing touch.

"You look stunning in that dress. I'm not sure you realize what kind of effect you have on men."

"Oh, I know."

"I thought we'd agreed that you wouldn't overdo this. We want Delaney to build a friendship with you, nothing more."

"Yes, that's the plan," I agreed. "But I have to fit in. I'll be at the Dry Martini tonight. I know what I'm doing."

"I know you do. I have something for you." He held out an ID with my picture on it, and then reached into his pocket for something else. "It's a new one, and here are some business cards."

I studied the ID. "Kendra James. I like it. Thanks!"

Then I turned my attention to the business cards. They featured my real name had a faint imprint of the symbol of the Resistance on them.

"What's this number? It's not yours."

He reached into his other pocket and pulled out a black transceiver.

I paused. "Guy..."

"Yes?"

"Would you like to be my backup tonight?"

"I thought you didn't use backup."

I looked away. "You can thank Eberhardt. He got me thinking about it."

"All right, I accept. You're the lead, so tell me what to do."

I thought a moment. Guy would need to look the part. He kept a couple of suits here, for when he stayed overnight. I walked over to the closet and pulled one out. "To start, you should wear this and bring this." I held up his black briefcase.

We arrived early. I went in first and chose a small table off to the side of the room as far away from the dance floor and piano as possible. Guy sat at the bar, ordered a drink and turned his gaze toward the dancers. He looked like a businessman who had just concluded a long day at the office.

I saw Brody Delaney before he saw me, so I stood to get his attention. He walked over and joined me.

"Hello, Brody." I smiled. "It's nice to see you again."

"How do we do this?" He started to hand me his briefcase, but I stopped him.

"Put that down. After a job well done, it's traditional to sit and have a drink first. We'll talk, and then make the exchange. There's really nothing to it."

He sat and placed the briefcase on the floor beside him.

"How do I know you're not really working for Cybonautics? I wouldn't put it past them, and this could get me into a lot of trouble."

"You're being paranoid. Why would anyone at Cybonautics hire me to do something that will only advance your career?"

He signaled to the waitress and ordered two martinis, one for each of us. As she was leaving, Guy walked by, stumbled into her, apologized and continued on to the restroom.

I put my hand on top of Brody's and commanded his attention with my eyes. "Brody, I think you've got what it takes. You saw an opportunity and took it. I think you'll make an excellent CEO at CalTech."

"I can only do that if you've done what I hired you to do." He spoke as if this had been his idea. That was a good sign.

"I have, and I hope you'll remember that Kendra James gets the job done."

"Kendra, now I have a name to go with your face."

The waitress arrived with our drinks. As she turned to leave, Guy stumbled into her yet again, on his way back from the restroom. I covered my mouth and giggled. Brody looked at me rather than Guy. He smiled too.

I reached out my glass. "I'd like to propose a toast...to new friendships."

Our glasses clinked, and we each took a sip.

"Do you like what you do, Brody?"

"I guess. It pays well. I didn't realize I'd have to be watching my back so much though. Everybody wants the top position, but everyone can't have it."

"I know what you mean. Those access codes you wanted? They'll help both you and your company get to the top, won't they?"

"Yes, they should."

The waitress returned then with an appetizer. "Oh, I didn't order..." Brody began.

"I did, before you arrived. Thank you." I smiled at the waitress who set down two small plates and a platter with artichoke dip and cubes of bread.

There was also small tracking device on the plate she set in front of me. I picked it up. "I hope you'll remember who helped you get to the top and that we'll be able to trust each other from now on." I dropped it into what was left of Brody's drink.

He looked down at his briefcase in alarm, then back at me. "Did I blow it?"

"Not yet. I can't fault you for being cautious, but I wouldn't try anything like that again. I am good at what I do. I hope you believe that now."

He glanced around the room. I was glad to see that Guy had already left.

"I also hope we'll be able to work together again sometime soon." I stood and held out my hand.

"What do you mean?"

I dropped my hands to the table and leaned toward him. Did I really have to spell it out? "There may come a time when I'll want to call in a favor from a friend at CalTech."

Brody looked at me in alarm.

"Don't worry. You could always say no. Until then, let's get together for drinks every now and again." I removed the list of access codes from my purse and handed it to him.

"That's it?"

"That's it, and to show you that I really am a nice person, I gave you a discount. I wouldn't leave your briefcase unattended until you've emptied it. Enjoy the dip." I picked up a small piece of bread, scooped up some artichoke dip, popped it into my mouth and swallowed. "Delicious!" I held out my hand again. "It's been a pleasure working with you, Brody Delaney."

-Scott-
Caught

Raquelle was now able to access the airport security systems. A week before we traveled, she removed my name from the high frequency list. She was able to get into another part of the system as well. There, she removed my army title from the database.

The day of our departure, Keira and I dressed up like a well-to-do couple going on holiday. Passing through airport security had never been so easy. The guards checked our IDs against their lists like always, but didn't bat an eye as first Keira and then I passed through the checkpoint. Guy would arrive on a later flight. We had all agreed that we shouldn't be seen together. It was risky enough with the two of us, though her new name lowered the risk some. We didn't talk much during the flight, anyone could be listening, and we arrived on time.

In the airport, we located a restaurant and sat down to eat. Guy's flight, booked through a different airline, was due to arrive only two hours after ours.

"What's he doing here?" I wondered aloud.

"Who?" Keira followed my gaze.

"Don't look."

She turned to me. "I'll be right back."

Before I could stop her, she stood and walked toward the restrooms. I looked again. He was pretending to watch the teleview at the newsstand. Yes, it was the same man who had followed April and me. *What's she doing?*

A few minutes later, Keira returned to the table with a magazine held loosely under her arm. She sat down and placed a call on her portable transceiver. I continued to eat while I kept a close eye on the man. He was still pretending to watch the news.

"Hi, it's Keira." She turned on the vidscreen briefly, just to verify her identity, and then spoke quietly. "I need you to check on a number for me. It's 49-73-60-41. Yes, I can wait. It's registered to who? With those codes we got, can you go into the airline databank, and change my name from Kendra James to Madeline Jones? Yes, as quickly as possible. I don't want to have to give up my new ID so soon. Thanks." She looked at me. "Elaine Ramsey knows we're here."

The man answered his transceiver, then walked away.

"He's gone," I said.

"She got what she came for then. That means Danielle and April should be safe."

"What did you do?"

"I checked his transceiver and returned it before he even noticed it was gone. He sent three pictures: one of you, one of me and one of us together."

"Then she knows you're alive."

"Without a doubt."

Just then, my transceiver buzzed, "I'll stop in tomorrow. Yes, that's the earliest I can manage." When I disconnected, I looked at Keira with concern.

"I've been ordered to return to base."

***

"You can't go," Danielle said firmly.

We sat in their parlor.

"I have to. I've been given a direct order by a superior."

"You don't have to," Guy corrected. "You could stay here indefinitely, but I think you should return."

"You think he should go back? To that, that lion's den?" Danielle asked.

"All Ramsey knows is that Scott and Keira are here, but we don't know what she wants," Guy explained. "She could have called Scott in at any time, but she hasn't. So why now?"

He had everyone's full attention.

"You said you were followed when you arrived with April."

I nodded.

"But Ramsey didn't call you back then. The only difference now is that you're here with Keira."

"That's right," Keira said softly. "She wants me, and we've known that for a long time."

"We have no reason to believe that she's aware of Scott's ties to the Resistance. You're right." Guy looked at Keira. "We can guess that she's calling Scott in to get to you."

April looked up in dismay. "Then Keira can't go back."

"Yes, she can," I said. "Just not with me."

"Then you're really going."

Danielle's face was damp with tears. I hugged her close. The others sat waiting for me to make the next move.

"We've worked so hard, spent so many years, getting people into the right positions so we could accomplish the most good. I can't let one person chase me into hiding."

With my sleeve, I gently wiped away Dani's tears. Then I looked at the others. "We need some time alone." We stood, and I led her down the hall to the kitchen. A few minutes later, we heard the front door close.

-April-
Art Fantastique

"Where to?" I wiped away my own tears. "What would you like to see?"

"I'm not really in the mood for sightseeing," Keira said.

"How about Art Fantastique?" Guy suggested.

I looked at him. "The shop is open right now. There would be customers around."

"That's all right. Let's show Keira what you'll be doing when you return to Tkaron. Then we can go to a restaurant or to a park...somewhere we can talk."

"All right. Follow me." I led them to a busy street a few blocks from the house. There, I was able to hail a cab.

I knew Keira's mind was elsewhere. Even so, as I gave the tour and explained some of the artwork that we had for sale, she acted impressed. I took them into the back room and shared a little of what Dani had begun to teach me.

"We were told that these two paintings were created by the same artist, a man named Pierre-Auguste Renoir. But you can see that the lighting in this one is significantly different than in this one. Since the first has already been authenticated, we know the second isn't an original," I paused. "Sometimes, it isn't so easy though. See these?" I walked them over to another set of paintings. "These three paintings: Lamppost, Central Park and Birds at Topock Marsh, were all created by a woman named Chen Chi. They look very different don't they?"

Guy nodded, and Keira looked at me with...was that pride?

"What?" I said.

Keira smiled. "I'm just really happy for you. This is the perfect job for you, isn't it?"

"Yes, I think it is." I turned to Guy. "Thank you so much for giving me this opportunity."

He put his arm around Keira and said, "I'm glad it's working out for you."

"There's a small café just down the block. Would you like to get some coffee or tea?"

Keira nodded, and Guy said, "Yes, that would be fine, Aimee."

I was starting to like the sound of my new name.

We sat outdoors at a table with a colorful umbrella spread overhead. Keira asked some of the same questions I had when I first arrived, and Guy's responses were very much like Scott's.

"How is it that the Mediterrans are so much more advanced than us? I mean, just look at all of this: hovercars, maglev trains, inexpensive and reliable public transportation..."

"Energy pulse showers that clean and massage."

Keira raised her eyebrows.

"No water needed. And safe food for everyone," I finished.

"How is this possible? Is it like this everywhere except Terene?" Keira looked to Guy for an explanation.

"No, not everywhere. Some other realms are faring poorly due to natural disasters like earthquakes and tsunamis. A few, like Mediterra, are doing really well. As far as I can tell, there are only two realms where a large percentage of the population is kept down. And only in Terene is the Divide caused by wealth or lack thereof."

"But why aren't people fighting back? I mean look at how life could be. It could be good for everyone!"

Guy shrugged. "The people who would fight aren't shown this." He waved his arm at the expanse of city in front of us. "They don't know how it could be. Think about it, only the Elite have easy access to modern techno, and no one in Terene has anything close to what every citizen has in Mediterra."

"Then that's the answer," Keira said. "That's what the Resistance should be doing. We should be working to educate people."

I knew what Guy was going to say because Scott had already explained it to me. "Someday, Keira. That's the goal. For now, although our convictions are strong, our numbers just aren't high enough to start a revolution. And unfortunately, we don't have an easy way to educate everyone. You have to remember that our economy is still recovering from the war. Leaders in the Gov use fear to justify their decisions and control the population. They've set it up so that every single person is trying to get ahead by stepping on each other, when the only real way to make progress is to band together and cooperate."

There was something more pressing on my mind. "But what do we do now? About Elaine Ramsey, I mean."

Guy looked at me. "Nothing. Other than Scott

leaving early, we'll stick to the plan, and in a few days, Keira and I will fly back." Keira reached out and took my hand as Guy continued, "Whatever happens after that, you'll stay here with Danielle. Let us worry about events back home."

-Scott-
Returning to Tkaron

Both Elaine Ramsey and Major Phelps were waiting to greet me when I arrived at the airport. A few other soldiers milled around and pretended they weren't here for me. I saluted and stood at attention.

"Follow me." Major Phelps turned on his heel. I fell in line. Elaine Ramsey followed. The major led us into a small grey conference room. He stopped suddenly and turned toward me. I heard the door close but kept my attention on the major.

"Sgt. Maddock." Major Phelps spoke in his familiar deep rumbling voice. I'd served under him for many years. He knew how to lead and was well respected. However, he was not part of the Resistance. "I'm glad you decided to return."

"Those were my orders, sir."

"What were you doing in Mediterra?"

"I went on holiday, sir."

"You didn't have permission."

"No, sir. I did not request leave."

"And where is the young lady?"

"She decided to finish her holiday without me."

He sighed and looked down for just a moment. "Under normal circumstances, I would order an investigation into your activities overseas."

The major and I both knew the Mediterrans would never allow the Terenian military to run an investigation in their realm. They would do it themselves, and even with the agreement between the Resistance and their President, they would have to look like they were making an effort. Cover ups could be messy.

"However, these are not normal circumstances, and we seem to have plenty of evidence without the hassle of an investigation." Major Phelps opened a manila folder and reviewed some papers. "You've traveled to Mediterra on more than a few occasions during the past three years."

"Yes, sir. Usually under orders."

"I see that some of these orders were issued by me," he paused and studied me carefully, "but I don't recall having issued them."

I didn't respond.

"Well, Sgt. Maddock. It appears that we have a traitor in our midst."

I did not look away.

Elaine Ramsey stepped forward and placed a document on the table. "I'm prepared to offer you a deal. If you sign this and give yourself over to Ramsey Corps, you will be honorably discharged, and no further disciplinary actions will be taken."

I read the document and picked up the pen.

-Guy-
Missing

We'd returned to Tkaron over a week ago only to find that Scott had disappeared. After two days, I called him. When he didn't answer, I left a message.

"Sgt. Maddock? This is Mr. Burke. I'd like to meet with you, if you have the time. There have been some updates to your portfolio we should discuss."

When he hadn't returned my call by the sixth day, I used a public transceiver to make another call. I kept the vidscreen turned off.

"Sgt. McGraw?"

"Yes?"

"Call me."

20 minutes later, my secondary transceiver buzzed. This line was secure and was rarely used. I turned on the speaker and vidscreen.

A woman in uniform appeared. "Guy Bensen?"

I nodded. "Thank you for returning my call. Maddock said you were my link to the military if anything were to happen to him."

"I've been expecting your call."

"Do you know where he is? I haven't heard from Scott in over a week."

"The last I heard, he was on his way to Parisio. I

figure something must have happened, and he decided to stay."

"No, I was there with him. He received orders to return to base, and he did, the very next day."

"He may have received orders, but he never returned to base. I checked the records when we were told he'd gone AWOL. The funny thing is, there have been no orders to search for him. With his rank and the number of years he's put in, that's odd. I thought maybe whoever was looking for him knew he was already overseas, but if he came back whoever wanted him probably has him."

"It's Ramsey."

She let out a low whistle. "If Ramsey has him. There's not much we can do, not without blowing our cover."

"Do you know where she may be keeping him?"

"I'd guess the Ramsey Corps lab, but I don't know how you'll get in there."

"I need you to do something for me, Sergeant. Be my eyes and ears on the inside. Contact me immediately if you learn anything."

"Yes, sir!"

***

Waiting was mentally exhausting. April and Danielle hadn't heard from Scott either.

I kept a regular schedule at the firm, and Keira spent her days training with Eberhardt and Ricardo. But every evening, Keira and I talked in circles.

Why had Elaine Ramsey taken Scott? To get to Keira. But that wasn't working, so why was she keeping him? And why did she want Keira anyway?

It was late, and once again, I was having trouble

settling down. Keira brought over two glasses of wine. She handed one to me.

"No, we need to keep sharp."

But she was insistent. "Don't kid yourself. You're not sleeping, your mind is constantly going. You need to relax."

"Have you been able to relax?"

"I'm trying to!" She held up her nearly empty glass.

After four glasses of wine, I fell into a fitful sleep filled with disturbing dreams. I was chasing people, trying to get them to safety, but one by one as I reached them, they'd disappear. I could do nothing to help.

-Keira-
Who to Trust?

I woke. Dim grey light filtered through the drapes. *Something isn't right.* I nudged Guy, gently at first, then harder. *Someone is here.* I couldn't wait any longer. I kicked Guy hard as I reached for the gun on the bedside table. He finally stirred. I rolled off the bed, dropped to a crouch and aimed at the bedroom door. Staying low, I moved toward the closet.

The door crashed open. A gun appeared first. It pointed at the bed, at Guy. He sat up and raised his hands in surrender. Two figures appeared in the doorway, both wore special ops uniforms. One continued to aim at the bed while the second scanned the room.

I pointed the handgun at his heart. *Are they here for Guy or for me?*

The soldier saw me but didn't shoot.

"Hold your fire!" Guy said.

What's he doing?

"Guy Bensen?"

"Sergeant McGraw." He nodded to the soldier on the right.

"Where's Richard Burke?"

"You're looking at him."

She lowered her weapon. "The girl..."

Guy lowered his hands and stood up. "She's not your enemy."

"Over here, sir!"

Sgt. McGraw took in the situation. Her man was in full uniform and probably wore a bulletproof vest, while I had on only a pair of lacy underwear, a tank top and my gold pendant. I raised my gun and aimed between the soldier's eyes.

Guy turned and looked at me. "Keira, put down the gun."

Sgt. McGraw ordered, "Private, you too."

He lowered his gun but didn't look away.

I backed into the closet. Only when I was out of sight did I lower my weapon.

"Stand down!" I heard Sgt. McGraw call out. *How many of them are there?*

I emerged a minute later. I'd slipped on a pair of jeans and fitness shoes. Guy wore the clothes he'd left in a pile by the dresser the night before, grey slacks and a black t-shirt.

-Guy-
The Real Question

Sgt. McGraw looked from Keira to me. "You called her Keira." It wasn't a question.

"Yes. Keira Maddock."

"Of course she is." McGraw leaned through the door and gave some orders to her men. "Nemes and Davis, guard the door. No one comes in, no one goes out. The rest of you, hold tight."

The sergeant stared at Keira. I knew she was noting the resemblance in Keira's bright green eyes.

"Our orders are to bring in Richard Burke for questioning. The charge is, 'unknowingly harboring a criminal.' You've been seen with Madeline Jones." She tilted her head toward Keira. "She's the one Ramsey wants. Madeline Jones is a known Freelancer. We have quite the dossier on her. You wouldn't know anything about that, would you?"

I looked at Keira. "Not a word," I advised. Then I turned my attention to the sergeant. "This is Keira Maddock, Scott's sister. Ramsey has been after her for a while. The real question is, does she know that Keira is also one of us?"

McGraw looked at Keira's pendant. "Is this a new development?"

"That's not the real question." Keira looked at me and completely ignored Sgt. McGraw. "The real question is why?"

"My orders are to bring you in, dead or alive," McGraw continued. She was still looking at Keira.

"But why?" Keira asked me again.

"Yes, why?" I said. "Why does Elaine Ramsey want you? We're missing something."

Sgt. McGraw gave up and leaned against the wall.

"We thought it was because you outsmarted her, but what if she outsmarted you?"

"What? No. She didn't play me. I approached her."

"I thought you said Scott told you about that job. What if she played both of you?"

"At one point I thought she was testing me, but it didn't make any sense. Why would she do that if she'd already hired me?"

"But she didn't pay you for that job, so why did she really want you?"

"So I'd have to do her bidding for free."

"She can afford your fees, easily."

"To get to Scott..."

"Scott is already one of her soldiers. He's had to follow her orders ever since her husband died." I hesitated. "Did you have anything to do with Curtis Ramsey's death?"

"No, I thought he died from natural causes."

"That's how it was reported, but I had to ask."

"She's probably after you and Scott."

"What if we're wrong? What if Ramsey doesn't have any real leads about who is who in the Resistance? What if she wants you for some other reason?"

"Then we're back to the beginning. Why?"

Yes, why? "Keira, you once told me that Scott asked you to join the military. Why didn't you?"

"Because I wanted to keep my independence. Scott said I could easily pass the same tests he had, but because of the rumors I..."

"The rumors about genetic screening?" I interrupted.

"Yes, and rumors about Ramsey Corps crossing the line."

"Keira, when I first met you, you had scars. Will you show them to us?"

"What? Why?" She pulled aside the short sleeve of her tank top. The skin was smooth and soft. Next, she ran her hand over her wrist and looked at it. She glanced up in alarm, then turned and lifted her tank top. She looked over her shoulder.

I ran my hand up and down her back. "They're all gone." She lowered her tank top. I put my arm around her shoulders, and together we faced Sgt. McGraw.

"Sergeant?"

Sgt. McGraw shook her head. "I know what you're going to ask, and the answer is, I don't know."

"What do you know?"

"Once a month, the doctors take blood and tissue samples from all of the special operatives. The samples are sent to the Ramsey Corps lab on the outskirts of Tkaron. I know the location, but I don't have clearance."

"Do they ever give you injections?"

"Yes, of course, vaccinations. And Special Ops are sometimes given other drugs to help us perform."

"What kinds of drugs?"

"They improve our speed, strength and endurance."

I thought about Keira's missing scars. "When you're injured, do you heal quickly?"

She pondered that. "Yes."

"How quickly?"

"Let me think. Pulled muscles are usually better the next day."

The other soldier spoke up. "When I broke my arm last year, it healed completely in just under a week."

Keira and I looked at each other in surprise.

"Who are the head doctors at Ramsey Corps?" I asked.

"There's Dr. Renaldt, Dr. Grere and Dr. Ross."

"Dr. Ross?"

Keira looked at me in alarm. "Isn't he the one who checked April?"

I nodded.

"He gave her an injection! But...he didn't give me one."

Another missing piece. "Did you eat or drink anything when you were at Ramsey's party?"

"No, but..."

"What?"

"I drank some tea she offered me, just a couple of sips. It was the day after I met you."

Keira put her hand to her side, then she hurried into the kitchen. The soldiers watched as she walked by. Sgt. McGraw and I were the only ones to follow her. By the time I realized what Keira was doing, it was too late to stop her. She had grabbed a steak knife and cut her left arm. Blood gushed everywhere, and the knife clattered into the sink.

I ran to a drawer and pulled out a clean towel. I pressed it against the wound. Keira put her hand on top of mine.

"Guy, let go," she said softly.

I did as she asked. Gently, she peeled back the towel and then wiped the blood off her arm. There was no cut.

She looked up at me with tears in her eyes. "What did they do to me?"

-Keira-
What Ramsey Corps Did

Injuries...Lance Beckett. He'd stabbed me in the side when I'd moved in to cut his throat. I'd ignored the pain because I had to get April to safety. Yet less than an hour later, when Guy noticed the injury, there was hardly a scratch. I'd convinced myself then that the blood at my waist had been from a small surface wound. Clearly, I wasn't hurt.

Now I knew. Something about me had changed. This cut was deep. I should have needed stitches. To say I could heal quickly...well, that was the understatement of the year!

I understood the value to Ramsey Corps. Imagine having strong, well-trained soldiers who could heal within seconds. As long as they were on your side, it was perfect.

So, why had she done this to me? I'd never been on her side. I thought about our last conversation.

"Keep in touch, Keira," she'd said. "I may require your services in the future."

Had she really believed she could control me? Yes, she had. And when she realized she couldn't, she tried to eliminate the threat. Even with rapid healing, I doubt I would have survived the blast at my apartment.

I looked at Guy, and tears welled up in the corners of my eyes. "What did they do to me?"

He took both of my hands in his. "I don't know, but we'll find out."

"What about Scott? What do you think they're doing to him?" I spoke so softly I could hardly hear my own voice, but Guy heard.

He pulled me close and held me tight. "We'll get him back."

Then he looked at the sergeant. "We're going in today. Can you clear the way?"

McGraw nodded.

Guy contacted Eberhardt and asked him to put together a team. They would meet us at safe house four within the hour.

McGraw briefed her men: Guy Bensen and his team would be breaking into the Ramsey Corps lab within the next few hours.

"If you are questioned about our mission here, you will report that no one was home when we arrived. Is that clear?"

"Yes, sir!" a chorus of voices rang out.

"If you are called upon to assist at the Ramsey Corps lab, your primary objective is to protect the intruders. Is that clear?"

"Yes, sir!"

"All right men, this is for the Resistance. Let's spread the word."

-Guy-
The Plan

As we neared the safe house, I made another call. This one was vital. "Can you meet us at safe house four? It's an emergency."

When we arrived at the little yellow house, three people were waiting in the living room. They stood as we entered.

"Eberhardt. Murphy." The burly men seemed to fill the small room. I would trust either one of them with my life. Then I turned to the woman. She was tall and slender with long shiny black hair pulled back into a ponytail.

"Ricardo?"

She held out her hand, and I accepted the handshake.

"Raquelle," she said.

"It's nice to meet you, Raquelle."

Just then the door opened and another couple entered. I hurried over.

"John. Alexis. Am I'm glad you're here!"

Alexis grinned. "You have a story for me?"

I motioned for her to sit, for everyone to sit. Then I began. "About an hour ago, soldiers broke into my apartment."

Eberhardt glanced at Keira.

"They're on our side, and with their help, we pieced together something terribly disturbing. Ramsey Corps has been committing crimes against humanity, and we don't have a minute to lose if we're to have any hope of stopping them."

I looked at my team. "Murphy. Keira. You'll be in charge of getting all of us in and out of the Ramsey Corps lab safely."

Keira sized up Murphy. He was almost as big as Eberhardt, a real muscle man. It occurred to me then that this would be her first real opportunity to work with a larger group, including a number of people she'd never met before.

"Raquelle, you're our high tech expert. We may need your help getting through security, but once we're in, the most important part of your job begins. We'll need whatever information is being stored on the internal Ramsey Corps system."

I turned my attention to Alexis, a beautiful and brave woman who not enough people recognized. "I'd like you all to meet Alexis Palamara, world renowned investigative reporter. Most of her stories never air in Terene, but I have a feeling that what we're about to discover at the Ramsey Corps lab will interest people everywhere. This could be an impetus for change. We may finally have enough evidence to wake people up."

I smiled at the tall red haired man who sat next to her. "And this is John Maes, biophysicist. His job will be to validate what we find in there. I'll likely need your help afterward to check through the information Raquelle recovers."

John nodded.

"Eberhardt, you're on double duty. First, I'll need

you to babysit. We'll be bringing along someone whose best interest will not be to help us. It's your job to make sure he cooperates. Second, depending on what we find in there, I may need you to destroy the place. Did you pack enough for that?"

He nodded. "It's in the car."

Just then we heard another car pull into the drive. "Eberhardt, please welcome Dr. Ross."

Eberhardt stood and moved to open the door. When the doctor saw all of us, his eyes went wide, and he took a step back. Eberhardt's gun convinced him to join the group.

-Keira-
Modified

"There's something you all need to see," Guy said. He looked at me, and I nodded. I went into the kitchen and returned with a large bowl, a sharp knife and a few paper towels.

Then Guy turned to the others. "Alexis, I know you brought your camera. You'll want to turn it on now, but I'm trusting that you'll keep everyone's identity a secret. Can you agree to that?"

"You know I can, or I doubt you would have invited me here today." She removed some equipment from her bag.

Everyone else waited in silence.

Alexis aimed her camera directly at me, and I felt a nervous twinge. I'd never been vid-recorded before except by surveillance cams, but this was important.

Guy spoke to the group and to the camera. "What you are about to see was done without this young woman's knowledge or approval."

I raised the knife and once again, cut my arm. I held the wound over the bowl. Blood gushed, but only for a few seconds. I picked up a paper towel and wiped away the blood. There was no wound. Alexis filmed for a few more seconds, then turned off the camera and set it down. She and John both stood up and walked over to get a closer look.

John looked at Dr. Ross in surprise. "You've done it!"

"But what has he done exactly?" I turned to Dr. Ross, "What did you do to me?"

John answered first. "He's modified you at the molecular level, using nanotech."

"What does that mean? Is there something inside of me?"

"Nothing that wasn't there before. You're still you. He's improved your white blood cells so they're better able to fight off disease and heal after injury."

Alexis looked at John and said, "Can I have an interview?"

"Of course, but later, I have a feeling there's more." He returned to his seat and looked at Guy. Alexis did the same.

Guy looked at each of us before he continued. "Does there need to be more? Like I said, this was done without Keira's knowledge or approval. That's illegal, even in Terene, no matter what her social status. Furthermore, Ramsey Corps is trying to keep this project secret. Why? What are they hiding?" He turned and looked at Dr. Ross, so did the rest of us.

"We're not hiding anything. We're still in the early stages. That's all. We're simply not ready to present our findings yet." Dr. Ross turned toward me and took a few steps in my direction. He smiled. "What a gift you've been given!"

"A gift?" I glared at Dr. Ross. "People can accept or reject a gift. They're given a choice. I wasn't."

"But my dear, had you been given the choice, wouldn't you have accepted this? A person would have to be crazy not to accept the gift of healing, of life. You of all people should know that. Just imagine if this had been available to your parents."

I could only stare. He had no right to bring them into this. "You really don't get it, do you?" My father should have been cared for, but he didn't need this. He'd just needed antibiotics. And my mother...if my father hadn't died so young, she never would have been in the wrong place at the wrong time.

Dr. Ross continued to explain. "I'm working to save people's lives, to help people."

"Reliance on citizens makes us great!" I recited the motto of the realm. "We should all do whatever we can to help improve society."

"Yes, exactly!" Dr. Ross said.

Guy moved closer and stood next to me. His support was exactly what I needed. "Curing the sick and healing the wounded. We should strive for that."

Dr. Ross smiled and nodded in agreement.

"Even without their permission."

"But why wouldn't the sick and wounded want help?" Dr. Ross was truly at a loss.

Guy said, "Dr. Ross, taking away free will and independence...that is and always will be, wrong. Your tests have been done illegally and unethically. We will stop you."

-Guy-
Who Else?

Dr. Ross's grin faded. "It's all of you who don't understand. Can't you see how this will help people everywhere?"

Why were they after Keira? There was something he wasn't telling us. "Doctor, have you given yourself the injection?"

"No." He looked at the ground, clearly uncomfortable.

"Why not?"

"Unfortunately, not everyone's system accepts the treatment."

My heart skipped a beat, and my hands went cold. "Please explain."

"Only a small percentage of volunteers have had such positive results."

"By volunteers, you mean soldiers, don't you? Were they given an option? Did they know what was in the injections they were receiving? Were they aware of the risks?" Our earlier conversation with Sgt. McGraw led me to believe they had not been given an option, and they did not know the risks.

Dr. Ross said, "They gave up those rights when they enlisted. It's all legal."

"Who else? Soldiers, Keira and April, and who else?" I pressed.

"That's classified."

I nodded at Eberhardt who clicked off the safety on his gun and held it against Doctor Ross's head.

He faltered. "Curtis Ramsey. I warned him about the possible side effects, but he insisted."

"Side effects? Death is one of the side effects? And you gave this treatment to unsuspecting people? You gave it to Keira?"

"With her it was different. We weren't even sure the formula could be ingested. I didn't think it would have any effect at all."

"What about April?" Keira asked. "You could have killed her!"

"No, my dear, I think not," replied Dr. Ross. "You and your brother had already responded so well, better than any of our other test subjects. Coming from the same stock, April had a very good chance of surviving the treatment."

"Did you ask her for permission? Did she know what you were doing?" Keira asked.

"No, I didn't want to frighten her after what she'd been through."

A small sound escaped Eberhardt. He'd heard just about enough.

Dr. Ross nervously cleared his throat. "April's injuries were worse than either of you guessed. She had signs of internal bleeding. It was an emergency, and knowing that her chances of surviving the treatment were high...I really did mean to help her. Is she all right?"

Keira turned away. She was right. He didn't deserve to know.

I looked at the team. "Have you heard enough?

Does anyone want out?" The room was absolutely silent.

There was one more thing I needed to know, for everyone's safety. I pulled Dr. Ross away from Eberhardt and spoke quietly. "What have you told Ramsey about the Resistance?"

"Nothing! I'm a doctor, not a spy. Believe what you will, but I truly value human life. That's why I'm conducting these studies. Ramsey Corps is the best way to finance this project. Elaine Ramsey provides the means to further science. We're helping humanity."

"You're lying. You must have told Ramsey something, or she wouldn't know that April had been given the treatment."

"I never said Elaine knew about that. Per our agreement, I never document the work I do for you. Like I said, I gave April the injection to help her. Until I checked her blood work later, I didn't even know...not that it would have changed anything. Please tell me it worked. I need to know that they're okay."

I looked at Dr. Ross in surprise. "They?"

He nodded.

I'd have to tell Keira about this, but not now. Now we needed to focus on Scott.

-Keira-
Infiltration

We drove southeast toward the city limits. Raquelle sat quietly next to me. She fidgeted with the handle of her bag and squinted into the bright sunlight that reflected off the hood of Guy's silver automobile. Eberhardt and Dr. Ross sat in back. Murphy followed with the others in Dr. Ross's red sedan.

I slowed as we neared the main gates. Two guards stood silhouetted in the windows of the gatehouse. As we approached, I recognized their military uniforms. I pushed two buttons, and the front and rear windows rolled down simultaneously.

I smiled. "We're here for a tour with Dr. Ross." I tilted my head toward the doctor.

"Yes, of course," said the younger of the two men. He reached over to open the gates.

"What are you doing?" asked the other. "Have you completely forgotten protocol?"

Without hesitation, Eberhardt shot him. He slumped against the first guard who gently set him on the ground and then opened the gates for us. The young soldier looked directly at me, and his gaze traveled down to my gold pendant.

"I'm glad to be of service, Miss. I'll make sure the security vids are erased and disabled. You'll have no further trouble from the military personnel on duty here today."

"Thank you." His response took me by surprise. Sgt. McGraw had been true to her word. My belief that military personnel were as close to the Gov as one could get without actually being the Gov completely shattered once and for all.

Dr. Ross directed me to an underground parking area. From there, we walked. We kept our tools and weapons hidden or disguised, all except Alexis. John pointed her camera straight at her as she described the building we were about to enter. Raquelle stood to John's side. She carried her own bag of techno tools but looked like part of the media team. It was the same for Guy, only his bag was full of Eberhardt's explosives.

When Alexis finished her intro, John turned off the camera and held it casually at his side. Dr. Ross led our entourage into the building. Eberhardt followed close behind, and Murphy and I took up the rear.

The doctor led us directly to the receptionist, a pretty young woman in a blue dress. A few other soldiers were stationed at desks around the room working at their data processors.

"Good morning, Lisa. I'll be taking a tour through today. Would you please open the door?"

"Certainly, Dr. Ross."

Despite what the soldier at the gatehouse had said, I couldn't shake the feeling that this was all too easy. That's when I noticed Lisa's fingers moving toward two buttons. I spun behind her and held a knife to her throat. From the corner of my eye, I noticed that Raquelle and Murphy had pulled their guns and stood ready to protect the group. Eberhardt remained focused on Dr. Ross. The soldiers throughout the room remained intent on their work. It was as if they hadn't even noticed us.

I spoke quietly into Lisa's ear. "Which button are you going to push?"

"The one that opens the door," she said.

"Good choice!" I patted her on the shoulder.

She pushed a button, and the door slid open.

Dr. Ross, Eberhardt, Guy, John and Alexis passed through the open door and into the corridor beyond. Keeping my knife at the girl's throat, I followed. While we waited for Raquelle and Murphy to confirm that the soldiers in the front room were indeed with the Resistance, I moved Lisa into the first room on our right, a small examination room, and bound her wrists and ankles securely with cable ties from Murphy's bag. That's when I saw it clearly, the detail that had slipped into my subconscious.

"Your name isn't Lisa."

She looked at me in surprise. "How would you know that?"

I indicated her name badge. It read, 'H. Schmidt.' "Lisa doesn't start with an H."

A short while later, Murphy and Raquelle joined us. Raquelle smiled as she held up a mini data storage device. I knew this meant she had copied at least some of the information we needed.

We moved further down the corridor. A number of doorways led into more empty exam rooms. At the end of the hall, we had two options.

Guy peaked through a small window in the door on the left. "It looks like dorms." He spoke quietly. "There's an open area at the far end."

Then he turned to Dr. Ross and asked, "Why do you need living quarters on site?"

Dr. Ross looked incredibly sad. "We really don't at the moment."

I was beginning to think the man was insane.

The door on the right required both a passcode and authorized handprint to open. It was there that Dr. Ross finally took a stand.

"No, I won't open it. I really didn't think you'd make it this far."

Raquelle made her way up to the front and opened her case. She attached some wires to the keypad next to the door and pushed some buttons. Numbers, letters and other symbols flashed across a small vidscreen in quick succession.

"Put his hand on the plate," she directed Eberhardt.

Eberhardt tried to pry open the doctor's fingers, but they kept curling up again before he could press his hand against the metal plate next to the door.

Raquelle sighed and looked at me. "You still have that knife?"

I nodded and approached the doctor. Eberhardt pulled Dr. Ross's hand up and away from his body. He slid his index finger along the doctor's wrist and spoke in a casual tone.

"Just hack it off right here. We'll need the hand intact."

Dr. Ross's eyes widened with the grim realization that he was about to lose his right hand, sans anesthesia. His fingers popped open, and Eberhardt placed the doctor's still attached hand to the metal plate.

The door opened to reveal the central lab.

"Oh...my...God..." Alexis turned on the camera as

she spoke. She slowly panned across the room so that viewers would be able to see for themselves.

At first glance, I guessed this looked like any large hospital room. I'd only ever been as far as a reception room before because my father had been denied treatment. Maybe the others recognized the techno devices throughout the room, but other than a data processor in the corner, I sure didn't.

Boxes that looked like refrigerators lined the wall immediately to our right, storage for the tissue and blood samples they took from the soldiers, I guessed. Along the far wall I saw a row of small machines that projected amplified images onto attached vidscreens. Mysterious squiggly things split and moved around on the screens. To the far left were rows upon rows of clear boxes filled with some kind of fluid. Floating in the fluid, were human babies. Some were as small as my thumb. Others were as large as a small purse. Many were moving.

Despite my ignorance, even I could see that the "genetic screening" that Ramsey Corps advertised was just a cover. They hadn't just crossed the line. They had leaped right over it and sailed far to the other side.

Dr. John Maes was drawn to the babies, and I followed a step behind.

"Are they alive?" I whispered. I moved closer to study the tiny male and female forms in the clear boxes along the wall. There were 18 of them, all at different stages of development.

Alexis turned the camera toward John as he turned toward me. She caught him in the frame, with the containers of babies clearly positioned behind him.

"Yes, they're cloning humans," he said. "This was outlawed centuries ago, in every realm."

Four exam tables stood in the middle of the room. Two doctors faced away from us, intent upon whatever or whoever was on the exam table in front of them. What looked like an adult form was covered with a blanket on the far table to my right. Tubes and wires connected that person to even more mysterious medical techno devices.

At the sound of John's voice, the doctors turned.

Eberhardt grabbed Dr. Ross around the neck and aimed a gun at his head while Raquelle, Murphy and I all pulled our guns and pointed them at the doctors in the center of the room.

"What's that? Who's there?" It was the voice of a young child. He stood on the exam table so he could see what the excitement was all about.

I lowered my gun in shock. "Scott?"

Guy hugged me from behind and whispered, "That's not Scott."

"But it looks just like him from when he was little! I know I was even younger...but that's Scott."

Guy repeated, "That child is not Scott." He turned me toward the figure on the other exam table. "That's Scott."

-Guy-
Ending It

We had to bring this place down, and we had to work quickly. I started giving orders.

"No names," I said to the others. I was certain the doctors already knew who Scott and Keira were, and they may have been familiar with Alexis, but there was no reason to compromise the rest of the team.

I nodded to Murphy and gave Keira a little shove in the right direction. "Secure the doctors. Don't hurt them."

I looked at Alexis. "Get a few more close up shots of the embryos and fetuses. Then pack it up."

Next was Dr. Maes. "Take whatever you need to help her back up her report."

Then for Raquelle. "Get to work on the data processor, and make sure you've got everything. Then infect the server and bring it down from the inside."

Finally, I turned my attention to Eberhardt. "Bring him along," I indicated Dr. Ross. Keira finished securing one of the doctors. She saw where we were headed, grabbed the little boy's hand and joined us.

Scott had been secured to the bed. Wires and

tubes connected him to a variety of medical techno devices. From what I could tell, they were monitoring his heart rate and temperature, feeding him through an IV and removing waste with a catheter.

Scott turned his head toward Keira. The pain in his eyes, so intense...but he smiled at her. Keira and I reached out at the same time to release the straps that bound his wrists and ankles. It had been done to his left hand, so she saw it first. I heard her gasp, but when she looked at Scott, he shook his head and looked pointedly at the little boy. The child climbed up the side of the bed and looked directly into Scott's eyes.

"Hi, little buddy," Scott whispered.

"Hi!" the boy responded. "Do you hurt today?"

"Oh, just a little," Scott lied. "How are you feeling? Better?"

"Yep!" he said, then jumped down and ran over to watch Raquelle.

As soon as the boy was gone, Keira's face contorted with rage. She turned to Dr. Ross. "What have you done to him?" She lifted up her brother's left hand so we would understand exactly what she was asking. Scott was missing two fingers.

I leaned forward and gently helped Scott into a sitting position. The sheets dropped down to reveal a large gash in his abdomen. When I looked up, I saw that Alexis had ignored my instructions and was filming us: Scott's condition, our reactions and Dr. Ross's explanations.

The doctor backed away, but Eberhardt moved with him. "Calm down. It's not what it looks like."

"It looks like you're cutting him to pieces!" Keira hissed.

"We were ordered to test his limits. He easily

regenerated one finger in just over 24 hours. Now we're seeing if he can regenerate two at a time. And just look! He'll be fine." Dr. Ross had the audacity to smile.

"Did you give them permission to do this?" I asked Scott.

"There was no choice."

"What did they take from inside?" Keira asked.

"My kidney, for a transplant." He nodded toward the little boy. "I'm glad they did that. I just wish anesthesia worked."

"An unfortunate side effect," Dr. Ross mumbled.

The blood drained from Keira's face. She pulled out her knife and moved toward Dr. Ross and Eberhardt. I could see by the look in Eberhardt's eyes that he was not about to stop her. The doctor tried to take another step backward, but Eberhardt restrained him. *This is barbaric. They're monsters! But she can't...*

"Keira wait!" She hesitated. "We need to know more."

Dr. Ross tried to explain. "For some reason we have yet to determine, some of the organs in the clones start to shut down around age four. We tried transplants, but their bodies rejected them. Due to so many failures, we even shut down the cloning part of the program four years ago. That little fellow was the last. But your brother and you," he nodded at Keira and smiled. "Your DNA holds the key. You're the only ones who have been able to regenerate. You've made it possible for us to pick up where we left off." Dr. Ross gestured toward the unborn babies in the containers. "Their bodies won't reject the transplants because genetically, you're the same."

"They're all us?" she asked. She looked at the

babies again. "Me and Scott?"

"Yes! The smallest one is even an April."

Keira looked at Scott. "Did you know about this? I mean, before?"

"No, not until...how long have I been here?" He looked again at the little boy. "None of this is his fault, you know."

I held up my hand toward Alexis and her camera. "Turn that off!"

She did. Finally, she did.

-Scott-
No Other Way

April once asked me, "Do you think what Keira does is important?" Without a doubt, I do. Like April, I often wish there were another way, but the soldier in me knows that often what we wish for and what is necessary are two entirely different things.

The day of my rescue, Keira stayed behind with Eberhardt. While he set the explosives to take out the lab, she turned off the clone wombs one by one. We couldn't take them with us, they never would have survived, and we couldn't leave them behind. The inhumane treatment and testing of human subjects had to stop. So Keira stayed, and one at a time, she turned off the machines. Eberhardt told me later how she'd wept for each one in turn. In some twisted way, they were our children, our nieces and nephews. When they left the lab, Eberhardt secured the metal door to seal in the blast.

Prior to that, Guy suggested that we move the doctors into one of the examination rooms closest to the entrance, as far from the main lab as possible. Keira asked why he was sparing them and argued that they would just pick up their research in another lab somewhere else funded by some other corporation. Plus, she insisted that Dr. Ross knew too much and could not be trusted.

While the rest of the team returned to the main entrance, taking my four year-old clone with them, Keira and Guy continued to argue in front of the doctors. Keira could have just kept quiet and later, on her way out, finished them off without Guy's knowledge. I think she would have too, in the past. But she wanted this all out in the open. She would keep no secrets from Guy. In the end, they reached a compromise, and Keira demonstrated exactly what she would do should they choose to continue their research. Dr. Renaldt and Dr. Grere were then moved down the hall.

The soldiers at the main entrance had been cooperative. Everyone agreed that no one must discover their ties to the Resistance. One of the soldiers suggested that we disable them and restrain them with cable ties. I knew what he meant, but I was in no condition to help. And anyway, my main priority was to protect the boy, so Guy led us to the cars while Raquelle and Murphy took up position, raised their weapons and fired. It would hurt like hell, but we all knew they would heal quicker than most.

As we drove away, the young soldier at the gate finally sounded the alarm. A few minutes later, we heard the blast.

We returned to safe house four, but only briefly. Before we went our separate ways, Guy had words with Alexis. He wanted all footage of Keira blocked from her show. But Keira once again, disagreed. She insisted that Alexis be allowed to use the footage, thereby keeping the truth intact. If the truth would bring down Ramsey Corps, then that was what she wanted and to hell with any risk to her personal safety.

In the days that followed, I had time to recuperate. I also had plenty of time to think. *Guy and Keira are both headstrong. He tempers her anger, and she makes sure he understands when stricter measures are in order. They're a good match.* I knew Guy would always let my sister be herself. He'd let her have her say and let her make her own decisions. He'd ask her the right questions. He'd continue to be her guide.

-Keira-
Alliance

It was a Tuesday evening, about 6:00. The atmosphere was relaxed at the Dry Martini. My jade green cocktail dress set off my eyes and contrasted nicely with my short, curly, red hair.

"Good evening, Kendra. I almost didn't recognize you," Brody said as he sat down across from me. "You look beautiful tonight, as always."

He emanated confidence now and was turning out just as we'd hoped.

"Why thank you!" I smiled.

He took a sip from his drink and then asked, "Have you been paying attention to the news?"

I nodded. "To some of it."

"Have you heard about Ramsey Corps?"

I shrugged. "Didn't she disappear? And I think I heard somewhere that her company's ties with the military have been severed, but I'm not sure why. Can you explain it to me?"

Alexis Palamara's report had not aired in Terene, but it had aired in many of the other realms. According to April, it was big news in Mediterra, and Terenian Elite with family in other realms had begun talking. Their servants listened and shared the news with their friends and family. It caused a domino effect, so even though most Terenians had not seen the show, everyone knew about Ramsey Corps. Palamara's report had the effect we wanted. It was enough to bring serious pressure against our Gov. People wanted to make sure stricter regulations regarding human genetic modifications and cloning were put in place and strongly enforced.

Brody explained what he knew. "Apparently, Ramsey Corps went too far with their genetic studies. There've been reports that they were cloning people. Her disappearance has only added to the controversy, and the Gov is leading an investigation headed by their top agents."

"But isn't cloning illegal?" I feigned surprise.

Brody studied me carefully. Then he nodded. "That's why Ramsey Corps is in so much trouble, and now Cybonautics is being scrutinized as well. Ramsey Corps uses many of their products, plus the two corporations have always been open about supporting each others' ideals. They even help fund many of the same Gov programs, but..."

"But what?" I pressed.

"You already knew all of that."

I smiled brightly. "So what if I did? I'm glad to hear you know all about it. And, it's been good for you and CalTech, right?"

"Yes, problems for one have resulted in problems for the other, and CalTech has reaped the benefits."

"That's great! Didn't I say you'd make an excellent CEO? By the way, I'm sorry to hear about what happened to your boss. Heart attack, wasn't it?"

Again, Brody regarded me carefully and nodded slowly.

It had taken a little extra effort to make that happen, and Guy hadn't exactly been thrilled. But we were a team now, and I had convinced him that having Brody in the right position was exactly what the Resistance needed. Sometimes, when bad things happen to bad people, good things can happen for good people, and that is the way it should be.

"How are you enjoying your new position?" I asked.

"Oh, I'm getting used to it." He took a sip of his martini.

"Congratulations on your acquisition of the airlines. I'm sure CalTech will keep us flying safe."

"That's our goal." He smiled.

"So, we're in good standing, you and me, right Brody?"

"That's right. After all, I wouldn't be in this position if it weren't for you, would I?"

I didn't contradict him. "So, hypothetically speaking...if I wanted to fly someone to Mediterra discreetly, that could be arranged?"

"What happens if I say no?"

"Then I'll have to find another way to keep good people safe. Brody..." I took his hand. "That's not a threat. You can always say no."

His curiosity won out. "Who do you have in mind?"

"Just a man and his son."

"So you'll need two round trip tickets and no questions asked?"

"Two one-way tickets, actually, and one round trip. They won't be returning."

He thought about it for a minute before he came to a decision. "Yes, I can arrange that. I'll need their names."

I dug in my purse and pulled out a list with our fake names. I reached across the table and handed it to him.

"Henri and Giana Moreau and our son, Marcel. How much will it cost?"

"Your son?" He shot me a quizzical look. "But you'll be returning."

I nodded.

"Drinks and dancing every Tuesday."

I set down my martini and sat back in my chair. "Brody, I'm not available."

"I'm thinking like a businessman, Kendra. You will be returning as Kendra?"

I nodded again.

"Obviously you've been keeping a close eye on me. I'd like a chance to do the same. Think of it as a weekly board meeting."

"A weekly board meeting?"

"It's good to have friends in certain fields, don't you agree? You help me, and I return the favor. It's a business arrangement that I'd like to keep alive and well with no more money exchanging hands."

I smiled. It was fair, and dealing in goods and services rather than money was exactly what we'd been hoping for.

"When would you like to leave?"

"As soon as possible. That is, if you want me back before next Tuesday."

"How about Thursday, an 8 AM flight?"

"That's perfect. Thank you, Brody." I stood and held out my hand. "So...you wanted to dance?"

When I left the Dry Martini, Guy fell into place beside me. He laced his fingers through mine as we walked to the car together.

Canvas Skies

I sit up suddenly and feel the blankets fall to my waist. I grip them tightly as my hands begin to sweat. *What was that?* I reach for the bedside lamp and pull the chain. A soft glow illuminates my bedroom. I swing my legs over the side of the bed and sit, just listening.

"April..."

What could he possibly want at this time of night? Oh no! I begin to shake. I can hear his footsteps on the stairs. I stand and look down. I'm already wearing my uniform. *When did I get dressed?*

My door swings open with a bang. There he is – Lance Beckett stands in my doorway, with his leather belt in hand. As he turns to close and lock the door, I notice the handle of a steak knife sticking out of his back.

He turns and moves toward me, looming larger than life. Blood spreads in a flower petal formation on his white business shirt. I step back and back until the wall presses against me, and I can retreat no further.

My breath is knocked from me suddenly as I feel a kick in my stomach. I look down at my bulging belly in shock and realize that it's true. I'm carrying his child.

I bring my focus back to Beckett's face and scream.

***

"April! April, wake up!"

I screamed once more and opened my eyes. Scott was shaking me, and Mr. Beckett was nowhere in sight. *He's dead. He can't hurt you anymore.* Yet I knew that wasn't true. He continued to hurt me every single night. I let out a breath and shuddered. Scott sat back on my bed as I reached for my belly. It was still flat but wouldn't be for long. I pulled my knees up to my chest and buried my face in my hands. Scott waited for me to regain my composure.

Finally I looked up and reminded him, "You shouldn't use that name. What time is it?"

"Just after two. Do you want to talk about it?"

I shook my head as Danielle and Noah appeared in my doorway. She was wearing a deep blue nightgown that could almost pass for a dress. He was in his green cotton pajamas printed with giraffes, elephants and lions. Proceeds from purchasing those pajamas, as well as the stuffed animals that now lived in Noah's bedroom, went to support a large animal sanctuary in Afrik. Their natural habitat had been devastated by human actions long ago. Now that sanctuary was the only place in the world those animals still lived. Afrik, like Terene, was in rough shape.

I looked at Danielle and Noah, "I woke you too? I'm so sorry."

"You have nothing to apologize for. We're here to help you," Danielle insisted.

Noah walked over and placed his small warm hand in mine. He looked at me with a somber expression though nothing could diminish the brilliant green of his eyes. "Let's go get chocolat chaud, Aunt Aimee."

"What? Do you mean hot chocolate?"

"Mama says hot chocolate can help," Noah emphasized the end of Mama, giving it a Mediterran flair. He smiled up at Danielle, "And it tastes tres bon!" Although they'd only known each other a short time, Noah had come to adore Danielle and she him. As for Scott, well the two of them shared a special bond all the way down to their genes. They were lucky to have each other, all three of them, and I realized I was lucky to have them too.

I leaned down and hugged Noah. "Merci. Thank you. I think that sounds like a wonderful idea!" As we followed Danielle and Noah to the kitchen, I quietly asked Scott, "How are you coping? You have even more reason than me for nightmares." It had been less than three months since the Ramsey Corps doctors had cut him up for their own experiments. Granted, one of the cuts had been to remove his kidney for Noah, but the others...

"Yes, I have them too," Scott put his arm around my shoulder as he directed me to one of the kitchen chairs. "We all do."

"Mama calls them cauchemars," Noah explained. Then he joined Danielle at the stove where she was getting out a small pot. She pointed toward the refrigerator, and he retrieved the milk for her.

We sat at the dark mahogany table while we waited for the milk to simmer.

Scott looked at me, "You should talk about it. It can help."

"Maybe later," I looked at Noah. He didn't need to hear about my demons. "What about you, Kiddo? What are your cauchemars about?"

"The doctors wake me up and take me into a really big room with machines and boxes of babies, and I can see Daddy lying on a bed. And..." His voice has gotten so quiet. It's barely a whisper. "They're hurting Daddy."

He hopped down off his chair and hurried over to Scott for a hug, "And then you wake up, and you're safe and so am I." Noah nodded as one lone tear trailed down his cheek.

Danielle walked over too and gently kissed the top of Noah's head before returning to the stove to add chocolate to the warm milk. We remained quiet, each lost in our own thoughts about what Ramsey Corps had done. *It's scary to realize exactly how much is beyond our control.*

Danielle had returned to the table. She placed the first cup of hot chocolate in front of Noah. As she set the second mug in front of me, I looked at her carefully, "You too?"

She nodded, "My dreams start out peaceful. I'm in a familiar place with Scott," she glanced at him, and he held her gaze, "but then he's gone. I look all around, searching, but I can't find him anywhere. It's the feeling of loss that turns my dreams into cauchemars."

Noah looked at her, "But then you wake up, and Daddy is there."

Danielle ruffled his hair and smiled down at him, "Yes, I wake up and you're both here, and we're all safe." She returned to the stove for that last two mugs of hot chocolate.

"What about you?" Scott was the only besides me who hadn't shared yet.

"Oh, I have a great many nightmares. They're all different, but I talk about each of them with Dani when I wake, and they've begun to fade."

"What do you mean by fade?"

"They're either not coming as frequently, or they're not waking me up. Either way I sleep through the night more often than not and don't remember anything the next morning."

He looked me right in the eye, and I knew. I didn't know how he was keeping it from Danielle, but I could tell. Scott was lying, probably to protect her. *Does she prefer lies to the truth?*

Noah finished his mug of hot chocolate and started to doze in Scott's arms. He was still looking at me, "Your turn."

"In a minute," I looked at Danielle and nodded at Noah. She walked over and leaned down. Noah's arms wound around her neck as she stood.

After watching his family leave, Scott turned his penetrating emerald green eyes in my direction.

I shook my head, "I'll share when Danielle returns. What have your nightmares been about?"

He sighed, "Sometimes people in white lab coats are hacking off my fingers and toes without anesthesia. Other times, they're removing my internal organs in order to keep hundreds of clones alive."

"Hundreds?"

He nodded, "And sometimes, there's no one in the lab but me. I search in the adjoining rooms but can't find who I'm looking for."

"And that would be?"

"Noah."

I nodded. Scott and Danielle had taken the task of naming Noah to heart. He couldn't remain Clone #24 forever. He needed a proper name. They had decided on Noah because of its meaning – peaceful and long-lived – traits they hoped for in the boy. Then there was the history of the name. Apparently, there was a man named Noah from ancient times who had been a survivor of a great flood. Legend says he had lived to an extremely old age. Scott and Danielle were uncertain about Noah's future yet hoped he would survive to live a long and healthy life. He was the first of his kind, so there was no way to know for sure. Would his other organs fail just as his kidneys had? None of the others had made it past their first transplants, so there was still a chance for him.

"I thought you said talking about them would help," I said, referring to Scott's nightmares, "so why have you stopped talking to Danielle?"

"Because although talking about them was helping me, it was hurting Dani. She won't admit it, but I noticed an increase in her nightmares when I began telling her about mine."

It was as I'd expected. He was protecting her. I reached over and squeezed his hand. "You can talk to me then. Anytime."

"All right but you need to return the favor."

I nodded and began to describe my nightmare just as Danielle returned to the kitchen. They both sat quietly as I related Lance Beckett's most recent attack on me while I slept.

Danielle spoke softly, "Talking about it won't be enough for you, April. Have you made a decision yet?"

She was stating the obvious. And she had used my real name – Danielle, who had been using my new name faithfully since my arrival. It was simply too much. After weeks of knowing that I still wasn't free of him, I finally wept for myself. And I wept even more for the baby.

"I don't know what to do," I sobbed. "Every night I relive what he did to me in one way or another. I just don't think that's going to stop once the baby is born. Seeing him or her everyday... What if it looks like him? This child deserves a clean start and lots of love, but what if I just can't provide that?"

"You could leave the child in Mediterra when you return home," Scott suggested. "Do you think the distance would help you to forget or at least move on?"

"Maybe, but I can't do that."

"Why not?"

"Because of what they did to me! Dr. Ross gave me the injection too. This baby will be able to heal and regenerate, just like you, just like me."

"April..."

"Aimee," I insisted.

He nodded as he spoke, "You don't know that for sure."

"Yes, I do." I looked directly at Scott and watched as realization of what I'd done spread across his face.

"You didn't. Not to the baby..."

Okay maybe he hadn't understood exactly, "No," I shook my head, "but I have checked. I can regenerate the same as you, and this baby is sharing my blood right now. The chances are high that he or she is like me, aren't they? I can't just give the baby up for adoption to some unsuspecting couple. What will happen to their child when they realize? The tests, the studies... I can't let that happen."

"There is another option." Danielle spoke so quietly that I almost missed it, but it was there, hanging in the air between us.

"No, I could never."

"Not that," Scott interrupted. I looked up at him, at them. What were they talking about? Scott reached for Danielle's hand. "We've talked about it, Aimee. We'd be happy to welcome your baby into our strange little family."

"Really?"

They both nodded, and I cried even harder than I had before, only this time there was a difference. These were tears of relief. I reached across the table. They each took one of my hands in theirs so that we formed a circle. It was a circle of protection, a circle of love. It was exactly what I wanted for my baby and what I feared I couldn't provide.

"When would you need to know?"

Danielle responded first, "Whenever. You can even wait until after the birth if you'd prefer."

I nodded. She was absolutely right. There was no reason to rush. I had months to decide. A sense of calm settled over me.

About the Author

S. L. Wallace is a full time teacher in an upper elementary Montessori classroom; a full time parent of a creative, story-telling daughter; and when she's not hanging out with friends and family, she squeezes in some time to write.

Interested in current events? Stop by and share your point of view and interesting links at CrossroadsOfHumanity.blogspot.com, or visit Sarah L. Wallace on Facebook.